Hell Rider

Hell Rider

GIFF CHESHIRE

Sagebrush
Large Print Westerns

Library of Congress Cataloging-in-Publication Data

Cheshire, Giff.
  Hell rider / Giff Cheshire
      p.   cm.
  ISBN 1-57490-364-0 (lg. print : hardcover)
  1. Large type books. I. Title
PS3553.H38 H4 2001
813'.54—dc21   2001032063

Cataloging in Publication Data is available from
the British Library and the National Library of Australia.

Sagebrush Large Print Westerns are published in the United
States and Canada by Thomas T. Beeler, Publisher, PO Box 659,
Hampton Falls, New Hampshire 03844-0659. ISBN 1-57490-364-0

Published in the United Kingdom, Eire, and the Republic of
South Africa by Isis Publishing Ltd, 7 Centremead, Osney
Mead, Oxford OX2 0ES England. ISBN 0-7531-6450-7

Published in Australia and New Zealand by Bolinda Publishing
Pty Ltd, 17 Mohr Street, Tullamarine, Victoria, Australia, 3043
ISBN 1-74030-307-5

Manufactured by Sheridan Books in Chelsea, Michigan.

Hell Rider

CHAPTER 1

HE SAW TRENCH DURNBO ACROSS OGALLALA'S MAIN
street, heading somewhere in a thrusting stride. Two
guns rode the Texan's hips, and a spoiling bitterness
twisted his face. As he turned away from the window,
Kelly Drake knew he might face those cutters before the
dawn of another burning day. Durnbo wouldn't be
satisfied until he'd tried his luck. Maybe the next time
that luck would be good. A man never knew.

Swinging about, Kelly scowled at the other men in
this hot room of Ogallala's best hotel. They had wasted
time he could have spent better wetting the dusty throat
he'd brought up the long and bitter cattle trail.

"Now, wait a minute," he said, temper roughening his
voice. "First you only wanted a man to clean a bunch of
rustlers off your range. Now it turns out you've simply
got a list of men you want killed off under that excuse.
Gents, you picked the wrong lobo in me."

He saw instantly that he had made himself some new
enemies. He had a way of doing that right and left.
Texas sang in his own blood. The bronco wildness of
the Pecos roared in his brain, and all the pugnacity of
the cow country was bunched in his hard brown fists.
His face was young, dark bronze. It held cold laughter
as he watched the three northern cattlemen pull up tight
in their chairs.

They'd said they came from the Standing Rock
valley. It was out in the sand hills somewhere, and
they'd made it clear that they threw the long shadows in
those parts.

Childress and Murchison were quiet men, caught in

1

some inner worry that kept them troubled and subdued. The one called Chance Comber was built on slight lines but looked plenty tough and sudden. His mouth had stubborn slashes at its ends, and the nostrils of his high-bridged nose were lively as a rabbit's. He wore a bushy moustache, a dab of chin whiskers and, more significantly, a six-shooter whose cedar grips showed plenty of polish. He'd done the talking.

"You take a dally on your imagination," Comber said now. "We're plagued with rustlers, just as I said. It don't matter a damn that they've set themselves up on coffee-pot spreads and pretend to be honest operators. They're burnin' our slicks and eatin' our beef and taking over the whole damned range. It can't go on any longer."

The other cowmen nodded in truculent approval of that statement. They knew Comber hadn't got anywhere with this Texan and weren't troubling any longer to hide what looked like bad dispositions all around. Kelly had known he was being sized up two or three times since he'd hit this shipping town, before they'd asked him up here for a little private medicine-making.

Too many people, he had learned, failed to realize there was a wide difference between a speedy and a hasty use of a Colt .45. His outfit had experienced a little business with horse thieves just south of town. He'd done some shooting, and the affair had been wound up, he'd hoped. But it had turned out they were three of the country's toughest ridge runners, which might have scared the hell out of him if he'd known it beforehand. Thus a reputation he didn't deserve, much less like, had preceded him to Ogallala.

These men had come to this railroad town to hire some Texas gunhands. Something they didn't know had misled them. He was about as lawless and go-to-hell as a man could get. But underneath that was a quality they hadn't figured on.

"Likely you've got a case," he agreed. "But you'll have to look elsewhere for your killer." He started for the door.

"Now, hold on," Comber objected, the bitter insistence still on his aggressive face. "If you don't want a hand in the rough stuff, all right. We can still use you and a few other rannies like you. We're going to vacate the land claims them rustlers have filed on, and nothing this side of hell can stop us. But we're still short of the men we need to grab 'em off for us, afterwards. We want to be sure we've got and can trust 'em before we make a play."

"How many such claims?"

"Around a dozen."

"Man, vacating them things takes more than a call at the land office."

"If we don't have what it takes, we'll get it." Comber reared back his head as his gaze drilled up into Kelly's. "It's that or we're done for. I'm telling you, them sons aim to carve us up. They make no bones about it. They're spoilin' for a showdown."

"Not with me they ain't."

"Good wintering job, Drake, and you said you ain't got one."

"And still ain't."

Comber's face roughened again. He said, "All right, buck. There's plenty of loose cowpokes in this town. We'll find our man. There's just one thing for you to remember. Keep your trap shut about this powwow."

"Any man tells me to close my mouth, Comber, and it kind of makes me talkative."

3

That was the wrong thing to say, and Kelly saw it instantly in the eyes that watched him. But he wasn't inclined to take it back. Again his own eyes laughed at them in a humor hard as winter light. Far off a train whistled, and he wanted to see it roll in. He wanted to erase the memory of fighting Indians, stampedes and the boiling dust of the trail. He walked to the door and went out.

Ogallala lay between the tracks and the river. It had a few liveries, a billiard hall, and a mess of saloons and dance halls mixed in with more sober stores and hotels. To add to its uproar now were the many big crews coming in with the beef herds from the south; dirty, shabby men with a lust for living in their sun-squinted eyes. Kelly joined the throng hustling to the depot to see the train arrive. It was a passenger from down the Platte, and Kelly got there just as it ground to a stop.

Jim Oliphant was already on hand, a lean, dour puncher who'd carried a worm in his brain on the long trail north. Kelly knew about Jim's trouble, who he hoped to find up here and what he meant to do. They'd been friends a long while.

Jim had a worried look on his face. He spoke in a lowered voice, "You step wide of Durnbo. He's likkered enough he wants to settle for that tongue-lashing you give him."

"Ready any time he is," Kelly announced.

"I'm telling you, he's made brags about what he can do to you. Looks like he's plumb jealous of the big rep them horse thieves give you. Them two cutters of his ain't there for nothing."

"A brag can cause a man a mite of embarrassment, Jim," Kelly said, and his unruly eyes decided Jim to drop the subject.

4

Then the eyes steadied—stared . . .

Kelly would have noticed the girl even if she hadn't stumbled over a rail of the side-track and gone down on her hands and knees. He was over to help her up only a second after she'd done it quite efficiently for herself. She started brushing off the cinders, so he picked up the valises she'd dropped.

"If you're trying to make that train, ma'am, you better let me help you."

"It's not the grips that dumped me. I'm just not used to these heels."

He couldn't even see the heels for the sweep of her skirts, which were plain, maybe a little shabby. But he didn't notice that so much as what was tucked away in them. She wasn't big, but what there was of her counted. She reached and took her grips away from him, annoyance gathering in her dark brown eyes at his reluctance to turn loose of them.

"Didn't mean to be fresh, ma'am," he said hastily.

"Texans never do."

"You don't like Texans?"

"Nor rattlesnakes."

She moved off down the dusty street instead of toward the train.

At Kelly's elbow, Jim said, "With Durnbo firing up for a fracas, you better not get women on your mind."

"I never get women on my mind. I got them there steady. You want a drink?"

"That's a want what I got steady."

They turned away from the depot and its throng, Kelly at liberty now to consider Durnbo. He'd hoped that they had settled their dispute back yonder down the trail. The set-to had come up over a horse, a company mount but one that had been in Kelly's private string. It

5

had eyes like a hoot owl and had for that reason been his favorite night horse.

But it was blistering mean when anybody forked it whom the bronc didn't happen to like. Durnbo learned of his unpopularity one night when he took the horse without Kelly's knowledge. When Durnbo got up out of the dirt, he quirted the cayuse half crazy. After Kelly got through lacing him down, Durnbo confined his meanness to his own saddle string.

Kelly didn't need Jim to tell him that Durnbo hadn't forgotten it. But he wasn't as impressed as Jim seemed to be by the man's two guns.

"Where you going when you've blowed your pay?" Jim was asking.

"South, I reckon. Mebbe lay over for another go at Dodge City on the way. After that, I dunno."

"After that, it'll be the grub-line. And you might as well ride it up here."

Kelly looked at his saddlemate in dark thought. "Jim, I've figured for quite a spell that you've got track of Linda and the baby finally. That where you're going from here?"

"I reckon," Jim said in a voice suddenly dull and flat. "It's what they call the Standing Rock valley. The town's called Lone Point. I guess I'll sort of pay a visit."

"And kill the man?"

"Mebbe try."

"Then take her back?"

"That's something I just don't know."

A thought that had started moving in Kelly's mind reached the surface. "Standing Rock, did you say? That's where Chance Comber and his cronies hail from."

6

"The goat-whiskered cuss that towed you up to the hotel? What did he want of you?"

"He's trying to hire a killer. Or some dummy squatters they need to put over a land-grab. Mebbe that's a good valley to stay away from, Jim, all around. Sounds like it's heating up."

"Speaking of goat-whiskers," Jim returned, nodding forward, "take a look at that."

But, even as Jim had, Kelly had already seen Chance Comber and Trench Durnbo come out of the Trail's End saloon together. They headed across the furrows of the street toward Comber's hotel.

"That time," Jim drawled, "he got himself a killer."

"And God help some poor greasy-sackers he wants to get rid of."

Again Kelly stared forward. A girl rode out of the livery archway just ahead of himself and Jim. He saw that she was the little package who had snubbed him at the depot. She wore a divided skirt now and fit fine where she met the saddle.

A stablehand, following her out, called, "Tell 'em hello out there for me, Abbie. Especially Badger Gamble. I ain't seen that old coot in a coon's age."

"He's been pretty busy."

Kelly blinked his eyes, something ringing sharp and clear in his mind. The nester leader, Chance Comber had said, was a man called Badger Gamble. The stableman's mention of the odd name hit Kelly like a kick of a horse. This Abbie must be heading for the Standing Rock country. The only decent thing to do was warn her that Comber had drawn up a dead list. But she didn't give him a chance. She was gone in a cloud of dust, heading out toward the sand hills and the trouble country. Somehow the situation he'd

7

been hearing about got more personal to Kelly.

Standing in the Trail End's scuffed sawdust, he had a couple of drinks with Jim. Afterward the lanky puncher drifted off, his main vice being stud poker. Jim was soon in a game at the far end of the room. Kelly's zest for the day was mostly gone, and he didn't know just why. He ordered another drink but hardly touched it, and this idleness soon brought him company.

She was a honey-colored blonde who had been built for a man to look at then grab for quick. In a voice to pull a bird out of a tree, she said, "Lonesome, cowboy?"

"Are you?"

She laughed. "Anybody who gets lonesome in this town has only himself to blame. Buy me a drink."

"Sure."

Most men just off the trail would have figured a girl in hand to be worth two in the sand hills, but he kept thinking of the one who had dusted out. She was bound to be on the receiving end of the trouble coming there if she was a close friend of Badger Gamble.

The honey-blonde had the drink that the apron set up for her, so diluted she could have drunk a gallon of such stuff without losing her cute little business head. She waited for Kelly to rise to the baits she kept shuffling around in front of him. Finally she snapped her fingers in front of his eyes.

"If you ever get back from that ride, cowboy, look me up."

She moved off, looking for livelier prospects.

Kelly turned and started for the door but never got there. Trench Durnbo came through the batwings with a noisy push. He halted just within, a long and leathery man whose weathered cheeks showed a heat. He knew what he was looking for, and when he found it his eyes punched holes in Kelly. He came on, still steady enough on his feet to be dangerous as a *brasada* bull.

"Drake," he announced as he came up, "you and me are going to tangle."

"That a fact?" Kelly inquired. "Over which of the dozen or so things we don't like about each other?"

"There's the matter of cussin' I took from you back down the trail for the good of the drive."

Kelly laughed. "Or till you could fill your belly with brave maker. Come on, and I'll buy you another slug."

"I don't drink with polecats."

"There," said Kelly, very slowly, "you've got a brand new matter, Trench."

"So I have."

Durnbo stood at a right angle to the bar, which had quietly but speedily cleared on either side, and he was out far enough to allow the free use of both hands. The guns on his hips loomed large.

"You boys simmer down!" the bartender rapped. But he was no novice in the shipping town and didn't protest again.

Kelly had both elbows on the bar, his right heel hooked over the rail, and he read the urge to murder in Durnbo's slate eyes. His chest rose under a dusty, faded shirt, and except for the tightening around his eyes there was no sign of disturbance in Kelly. Then he sprang from that idle position. His right fist hooked as it hammered into Durnbo's belly. The man expelled a blast of air as he went down.

Kelly was on him in one pounce, intent momentarily on getting possession of those two sixguns. When he had them, he placed them on the bar and turned, standing back. Every man in the saloon was on his feet by then, breathing a sigh of relief.

9

"If you still hone to tangle, Durnbo," Kelly said, "rise and shine."

Durnbo seemed to be even more of that mind as he boiled to his feet, humiliated at being disarmed so unexpectedly and forced to fight a different way than he had wanted. But he was game, and he came in steaming. His flicked fists drove Kelly back half a dozen steps.

Each blow hurt, giving Kelly plenty of trouble getting set. For some queer reason he was thinking of Abbie again, remembering what this gunhawk had probably hired out to do to her friends. He began to block Durnbo's blows, getting in lick for lick, forcing the man into a slow and panting retreat. His knuckles split on bared teeth when he sent the man crashing down.

"By God!" Durnbo gagged. "By God—!"

He got his feet pulled under him, staring upward. Then an arm flung up. Before Kelly could duck, he'd taken a whole handful of the dirty sawdust in his face. Blinded, he sludged at his eyes as Trench Durnbo hurtled up at him, punching hard. The man sent in a vicious assault, smashing Kelly against the bar with tears streaming from his dust-fouled eyes. There was a moment when Kelly felt himself giving way, going down.

Then enough clear light got through to his eyes to let him see his man. His face wore a twisted rage as he bored in. The first meaty impacts of his fists straightened Durnbo on his toes. But Kelly didn't want it to end easily. He followed the man half the length of the bar, kept hitting even after Trench Durnbo was helpless. Finally a single clean punch sent him down to stay. It would be a few days before the man would be in shape to murder anybody. If Chance Comber was impatient, he'd have to start hunting up a new killer.

Kelly wheeled, sick of it and sick from it, as well. The place was jammed with Texans and, like all gunhawks, Durnbo had his following. But mostly Kelly saw a look of gratification on the blurred faces about him. The others, mainly Smiley Dennis and Pete Koster who were Durnbo's running mates, were sullen but not aggressive.

"Everybody satisfied?" he gasped.

Nobody claimed to be otherwise.

He was sweaty, bleeding, and smeared from top to bottom with the sawdust. He was heading for the door, ready to call it a day, when somebody intercepted him.

It was the honey-blonde, who said, "Now you're acting more like a cowboy in town. Coming back?"

"Not tonight."

"Then wait a minute. There's something I got to tell you." She put a hand on his arm and looked into his face very earnestly. "Buy me a drink, and I will."

You paid for what you got from her, no mistake, and circulating the way she did she might know something worth hearing, Kelly told himself. When Kelly started toward the bar, again three-deep with customers, she tugged him in the other direction. She made a signal to a bartender, then Kelly followed her down the passage at the end of the room, into a private stall. The bar-keep came immediately with a bottle. Whoever she was, she apparently rated service.

When they were seated, drinks in front of them, the girl smiled at Kelly.

"You sure pack a wallop. I mean more ways than one, and it's got you into trouble, already. But you better have your drink, handsome. You're real green around the gills."

He didn't doubt that he was, for the reactions to

11

violence could take the sap out of a man. He was dull, jaded, and he tossed the drink off fast. She poured another, but he was cagey enough to let it ride a while.

"About this trouble?" he suggested.

"You know a man named Comber?"

He stared at her, getting duller by the second, and sicker.

"Not on intimate terms, thank God. What about him?"

"He's a friend of mine."

"That old goat? He must be a good spender."

"That's all it takes."

He was beginning to catch on, and he made a wild slap at the table top as he tried to get to his feet. But the room reeled and he fell back into the chair.

"About the trouble," the girl was purring at what seemed to be a great distance from Kelly. "Comber come to see me a while ago. About you, cowboy, and this . . . is that . . . trouble . . ."

But the whole thing had slipped from Kelly's grasp.

CHAPTER 2

HE LAY FOR A MOMENT WITH HIS EYES OPEN, LIFTING his head and looking at the sky, very blue beyond the hot, thick edges of his eyelids. But he couldn't look long and closed the lids as new agony wrenched his insides. Then he heard a clickety-clack and realized in slow horror that he was moving. It took his stupid mind seconds longer to figure out that he was on a train. From the brightness of the sky, when he could look again, this was a new day.

He sat up, sick and drunken, and saw that he'd been

thrown into an empty, open-topped gravel car. There was no telling how far he had traveled. That would depend on when the freight had rattled through Ogallala, which had probably been in the night. He remembered the yellow-head he'd let outsmart him and swallowed a bitter curse. The clacking wheels seemed to laugh at him. He could de-fang a Durnbo, then a slip in a silken sheath could pour knock-out drops down his gullet and him holding still for it like a lamb on a bottle.

He got to a groggy stand, holding onto the sides of the car. He stared at the unvaried plain of windblown sand and dunes, past trees that must mark the course of the river. He still had no idea where he was, and he scowled in the hard search of his aching eyes for some familiar landmark. None of yesterday's high spirits were left in him. A man could play the fool and, if he played it good enough, he could get killed.

He closed his eyes again and felt the pressure and streaky lights smear together in his mind. Had the towhead only rolled him? He looked wildly into his money belt and saw he had no need to be alarmed about that. She'd done what she'd taunted him with—helped Chance Comber despatch him from the country. He was lucky he hadn't been consigned farther, to the regions from which no man came back.

Kelly made himself climb the end section of the swaying car. Blood surged to his brain and blackness swept away the grass-patched sands about. He caught hold of the brake wheel and held on until the streaks jarred to a stop and became drab shapes again. He edged himself over and, with a groan, managed to climb to the pitching top of the box car behind.

Its roof was searing to the touch and already sweat leaked from his whole hide, a quivering sickness still tugging at his stomach. He couldn't stand so he crawled all the way back to the caboose. A look over the edge at the weedy sands streaming past arrested his impulse to climb down into the caboose. He sat there, swaying and sick, while the freight sped on. He tried hard not to think.

An hour later he could see, far ahead, the shape of a water tank against the burning sky. Soon a few huddled buildings disclosed themselves below it. The train stopped for water. A sleepy-eyed conductor came awake to stare at the man who staggered wildly into the caboose.

"Where the hell are we?" Kelly gasped.

"Who the hell are you?" the man retorted. When he had learned, he shrugged his shoulders. "Buck, you're a smart piece from Ogallala. Only thing you can do is get off at Kearney and catch the passenger back. Where you been all this time?"

"Tryin' to catch you," Kelly growled. He headed for the water keg he'd located . . .

The cayuse silked its hoofs slowly over the sandy trail. The sun was on Kelly's left, where he figured it should be if he was ever going to get to the Standing Rock valley. That hadn't ought to be far now. A fierce and burning pressure flowed from the brassy sun to scorch his whole side. Something vague and distant lifted his head. His horse threw its ears forward, then Kelly reined in. He could hear the faint, far beat of massed hoofs going fast.

Off to his right riders came up as if from a hole in the ground. They didn't slow as they broke over into view and followed the distant ridge ahead of him. They rode hard, the horses kicking a cloud of dust into the

14

rearward air. Then they dropped from sight to his left, as abruptly as they had appeared. There had been three of them, pressed men riding swiftly, not following the main trail. Chasing something or running from it? Kelly wished he knew.

He turned his horse toward the point where they had dropped from sight. Their tracks were still there, with the smell of stirred dust to prove he'd seen no phantom riders of pestilence, war and death, to which this Godforsaken country could easily give birth. He began to descend the far side of the slope, watching the land that presented itself beyond the ridge.

It had changed considerably, revealing to his tired gaze a larger basin than any he'd seen so far. There was a creek at its bottom, cottonwood on its banks. On the walls of the farther hills the heat of the sun was trapped, dusty and flat and arid as the earth itself.

Beyond the creek was a huddle of small buildings and corrals, colored like the hills so that he hadn't recognized them at once. The riders were bearing down on the place, still going at a fast clip.

Whoever lived down there was in for trouble.

The shock of the discovery cleared his mind of its bewilderment, leaving it alert, so that all the possible reasons for this piece of business streamed through it, swift and clear. This was the nester country now. Those riders were so surely business bent, it looked like Chance Comber had found the men he needed, and one might be a recovered Trench Durnbo.

The ball was ready to start. Kelly had bought himself a ticket to that function down in Kearney and had spent three days getting back to this point. He'd found his old outfit cleared out of Ogallala, with even Jim Oliphant gone. Then he'd started asking directions.

He stared downward, the impact of the blazing light rough and burning on his eyes and drilling into them with a sharp pain. As the riders drove in on the soddy, he saw a puff of smoke at the door. Seconds later he heard the dulled but urgent crack of a rifle shot.

His anger broke like an echoing crash as he watched the attackers return the shooting, coming in like Indians, flat as they could get on the backs of their running horses. But the brightness stung his eyes and he had to close them for a moment. When he looked again, the riders had flung off their horses and taken shelter. They were soon pouring a bristling fire on the sodhouse. He saw the smoke puffs as retorts came from the doorway. Then he drove steel into the flanks of his horse.

The cayuse caught his excitement and kicked sand as it started down the slope. When he came down into an intervening depression, he lost sight of the scrap, but his ears told him the shooting had stopped, at least momentarily. Scowling, he topped the next swell. It was over, all right—almost.

The three horsemen were back in leather. They'd thrown the loops of their catch ropes over the end posts that held up the roof of the soddy. As they hauled back, the poles gave way. The whole earthen structure collapsed in a rumbling cloud of dust. Kelly ripped out a curse, fearing somebody was still in that house.

They saw him coming, then, and swung his way. He heard the scream of close-whipping lead, the renewed racket of guns. He gripped his own sixshooter but didn't yet fire. They pressed closer, and he knew they figured to capture or kill him. From their work just now, they wouldn't care which it was. When he could do some good with it, he shot twice.

They'd come close enough by then for him to see

16

them all very plainly. His lips pinched tight. It was no surprise that they were Durnbo with his hardcase cronies, Smiley Dennis and Pete Koster. Their murderous work for Chance Comber was started.

He shot again, and Pete Koster, who'd come closest, jerked in the saddle, steadied himself and swung his horse about. Kelly's next shot forced the other two to wheel also and sent them driving away from him. When they had pulled out of range, they paused for a moment at the soddy. He couldn't see what went on, but when they drove out again, heading for the distant ridge, he thought that one of them carried a limp form across the saddle in front of him. Kelly couldn't be sure what it was.

The dust of the collapsed sodhouse was a thin smear in the hot air. As he rode on in, the sight of the place appalled him. The roof had been of poles and a heavy layer of dirt. The spreading walls had let it all dump into the house's interior. There was a heap of rubble and poles in the doorway, maybe more. They'd taken something away with them, but someone might still lie smashed beneath that heap, someone of quick fight and stubborn courage. If so, it would be somebody dead from that crushing, smothering cascade, and there was no hurry about digging in to see.

Between the ruined soddy and the bank of the creek, Kelly observed a well. It was open, with a gallows over it, and a rope showed the fraying of heavy wear. Walking over, he lowered the pail until he heard it splash hollowly, far below. The dead man, if he was still in that ruined house, had put in a lot of hours digging that deep. He looked around, seeing no livestock and wondered why anybody would fight over such a piece of real estate.

The well water, when he'd hauled it up, slopped cold and clear from the bucket, and his throat caught fire with thirst. He was about to drink when he stiffened, not daring to move a muscle.

"I've got a gun on you," the voice behind him said.

It was very familiar, not a man's, and he felt the shock of it climb his back. A quick, bright anger at his carelessness exploded in his brain. His hands were full of bucket, and he was tempted to whirl and throw the water. Yet, remembering the voice fully, he didn't do it.

He watched the shadow that slid out past his feet. It wasn't a big one and it moved slowly. A hand reached out and got the gun from his holster, and his downcast gaze showed the hand to be small and very brown. There was still a live shell in the gun, he remembered.

"All right," the voice said. "Turn around."

He obeyed and found himself staring into the muzzle of his own sixshooter, the only weapon she had. He hadn't been mistaken, and Abbie had bluffed him skillfully. She wore a calico dress, frayed, faded and shrunken, although the tightness didn't hurt her looks a bit. Her feet were in moccasins now, he noticed, below bare brown legs.

"Thank God," he breathed. "I figured you were either in that soddy or they'd lugged you off. How'd you get away from them?"

Her eyes were dull with shock. She was too tense to say anything just then, although she must have remembered him and seen that, just now, he'd helped her out. She stared at him from a face nearly as brown as her hair, and he was struck by the deadly, motionless rigidity of her body. Yet there was nothing hysterical there. Her eyes were strong, determined, and she wasn't afraid of him.

18

"What are you doing here?" she breathed, finally.

"Having a drink right now, if you don't mind. I'm some dry."

"Go ahead."

He tipped the pail to his mouth and drank heavily, spilling water, swallowing in long gulps. The liquid's sweet coolness cut the sickness lingering in his stomach from the dope. Its impact seemed to go all through him, washing out the excess heat of his tired flesh. He lowered the pail to the ground.

"Just who are you?" she asked then.

"They call me Kelly Drake. Like you guessed in Ogallala, I come up with a Texas herd."

"Another Texas gunman," she said bitterly. "Another trail devil—a hell rider looking for trouble. Did you make a mistake? This isn't a big cattle ranch. You pitched in on the wrong side."

"You're plumb off the track," he said hotly. "I know a two-bit cow outfit when it comes to that. And when I seen you shooting from the doorway, I bought chips in the game on your side."

"It wasn't me shooting," she said in a low voice. "But my father, Terry Kilrain. He made me hide in the barn when he saw them coming. I hope they killed him before they pulled down the house. If I'd only had a gun!"

"You got one now you don't need," he told her. "You'd best give it back. I had a notion they'd carried somebody away from here. Could you see?" She shook her head. "Then you better give me a chance to see if we can help your dad."

She looked at the ruins. "Even if he's in there, he's past help."

"Got a shovel?"

"There's one in the stable."

To his surprise, she lowered the gun, reversed and handed it to him. Maybe she still didn't trust him, a Texas man, but right now she had further need of his help. It made his flesh crawl to think what might have happened to her if he hadn't been on hand. They'd have searched the place and found her, and he hated to think of her helpless in the hands of Trench Durnbo, Smiley Dennis and Pete Koster. They'd nailed an Indian girl coming up through the Territory and bragged about it afterward.

She showed him where to get the shovel and stood by quietly while he started digging into the ruins of the sodhouse. They both were tight-faced and quiet. It took a long while to unearth enough of the floor, although Kelly worked hard and fast. The sod blocks were tough, and finally he had to start throwing them out one by one. Sweat streamed from him, and he was dizzy from the heat and exertion when he had finished the job.

"They took him away," Abbie said. "I wonder why."

"That's easy. You can't prove there's been a murder without a body to prove it."

She nodded, her eyes still dry and hard.

"You got what it takes, Abbie," he said, and his sincerity went deep. "You just arrived in this country?"

"Oh, no. Dad knew what was coming but kept it from me the best he could. He sent me off to Omaha, but I knew more than he thought I did. I just couldn't stay away, so I came back."

"I'm sorry," he said and felt foolish because it was so feeble a thing to offer.

"I hope you'll go to town with me," she said fiercely. "Your backing would help when I report this to the sheriff."

There was no sound for a moment except that of the hot wind moving over the sand. He looked at the girl, alert and pleading to him with her shock-filled eyes, standing stiff as she waited. He saw all the horror of the situation in which she had lived, saw the horror now. He didn't know much law but figured that she would inherit her father's homestead rights, which would put her next on Comber's dead list.

He'd come to even scores with Comber for those knockout drops but had figured on doing it in a more direct manner. If he got involved in a range war of which he knew little, there was no telling where it would lead. He could feel his pulses crash in his ears. It was difficult to sort out his thoughts and put them together the way he had to now. He looked at her steadily. She looked back, waiting patiently but now with a bit of distrust in her eyes. Then he felt the disturbance within him die down and suddenly his head was clear.

"Where's your horses?" he asked.

"We have to let them run loose. We haven't any feed."

"Just tell me where to catch you one."

"You'll come with me?"

"I don't think it'll do much good, Abbie," he said somberly. "But I'll help you all I can."

CHAPTER 3

THE TOWN OF LONE POINT, AS STARK AS THE COUNTRY that gave it being, lay hot and humid on a creek bottom. A ragged belt of cottonwood and willow broke the sameness of the land to lend here a rustic appeal. A single wide street, built for turning wagons, started from

21

the yellow prairie and ran on into prairie again, passing a score of hitchracks and wide open doors. On either hand, dwellings spread away in seeming disorder. It was like a hundred other remote cowtowns up and down the Great Plains.

Riding onto the street with Abbie Kilrain, Kelly had a sense of passing suddenly into a field of electric force he himself was helping to create. One by one the armed men on the walks turned to watch the newcomers, a strange cow puncher with one of the nester girls. What talk there had been died away. Men swung in intent scrutiny.

A man called, "Abbie—is something wrong?"

"Dad—they killed him."

Kelly felt as if he'd swallowed a prickly pear. It was midafternoon, a strong sun simmering on the sandy dust and bursting aflame on the eastside window panes. Abbie rode a good horse and held the reins so that a round, brown arm pressed tight in tension under her firm young breasts.

Men started to move along the walks abreast them, knowing now since they were going to the courthouse that a ghastly crisis had come. Across a vacant lot, as they passed it, Kelly looked out toward the gray shapes of the sand hills, scabbed with grass and runty weeds, looking as barren otherwise as the middle of an alkali sink.

Again he wondered what could have brought anybody here, why it was a land to fight over until blood ran and death smeared away what little goodness there was. But these men saw the values there in the free grass, he realized, and seemed to have no question about them.

When they came to a square, unpainted building distinguished only by being larger than its neighbors,

Abbie said, "This is it," and turned in toward the hitching posts in front. The men who closed in about them were all her friends, apparently, the others having uneasily dropped out.

A man caught her arm as she swung down.

"What happened?" he growled.

"It's a case for the sheriff, Ed," she said quietly. Her voice made the listeners subside.

She turned and looked at Kelly with clear, steady eyes in which there showed an unyielding determination and still no hint of fear. In this voiceless way she was asking if he was ready for what must be a difficult step. He was aware of the hard scrutiny on him because of his obvious Texas origin as shown by his saddle rig, his hat. His breath ran shallow, and his cheeks were stiff.

As he followed her up the steps he could smell the dry, pitchy odor of raw lumber and the stirred dust of the street, the hot, sharp scent of the air itself. Abbie led him past a couple of doors in the dark hallway they entered. He tried to swallow with a dry mouth, knowing this was a step that could not be reversed.

The sheriff's office was big and plain, bare except for some files and chairs and a couple of battered desks. There was a man at each desk, both staring at the doorway as if aware of the focused interest on the street. Kelly halted in his tracks when he looked at the younger man, who wore the badge of a deputy on his vest. He saw the jarred look on the man's face but neither of them spoke.

Abbie was looking at this man, too. In a low, tired voice, she said to the other, "Charlie, I'd rather talk to you alone."

The sheriff's mouth pulled longer, straighter. He glanced at the other man and said, "Excuse us a while,

Rio." The deputy rose, a look of anger on his face. A glint of suspicion added itself as he glanced again at Kelly. Then he strode out, heels and spurs clicking hard on the bare floor.

The sheriff, introduced by Abbie as Charlie Redd, was neither young nor old, big nor small—one of the countless lackluster officers who wore out their lives trying to keep law and order in a country that didn't seem to want them. Kelly trusted the situation better after he'd accepted the man's firm grip and shaken hands. They took chairs, and Kelly listened, letting Abbie do the talking.

Redd leaned back in his swivel chair while he heard her out. His slate eyes grew colder by the minute, beginning to streak with a strange, black light. Kelly could see out the window into the flaming heat of the day. Men still waited out there.

When Abbie was done talking, Redd threw up his hands. "I can't do a thing till I can locate Terry or his body. And you say the men were all strangers to you, what little of them you seen."

"Not to me," Kelly cut in. "I seen 'em close enough to know 'em for hardcases out of the outfit I come up the trail with. Namely Durnbo, Dennis and Koster. I think I hit Koster. If you don't pick 'em up, Redd, there'll be plenty more killing before you've found out what happened to Kilrain. I know them three. They're bad."

"Pick 'em up on what?" Redd asked. "Hold 'em on what? Mister, pullin' an arrest in this country's the same as pullin' a gun. You got to have some ammunition in either case."

"They destroyed property out there," Kelly said stubbornly. "The evidence of that is too much for 'em to remove."

24

Redd pondered that, then shook his head.

"Why not?" Kelly demanded. "They're working for Chance Comber. He tried to hire my gun in Ogallala. Whose side you on?"

"Nobody's," Redd snapped. "The ball's rolling, and I can't stop it by locking up three hardcases for destroying property. Building such a case would be clean off the trail, and somebody might like to have me tied up with it."

"What're you going to do, then?"

"Try and find what's left of Terry Kilrain." The sheriff looked at Abbie. She hadn't spoken since telling her story and sat straight and tense in her chair. A puff of wind came through the window, rank with the street smells of the town and ranker yet with the ugly tensions out there. In a kindlier tone, he said: "Abbie, couldn't you stay here in town a while? You've got me worried."

"I can take care of myself. And thanks, Charlie. I know you'll do what's best."

If she felt that way, Kelly reflected, then he might as well.

Charlie Redd gave him a long, searching study, then said, "You aim to be around a while? If not, be sure and let me know how to get in touch with you. If I can ever put together a case, I'll sure need you."

"Dunno what I'll do," Kelly said impatiently. "But if I decide to pull out, I'll tell you."

Abbie left town immediately with an escort of nesters strong enough to give a band of wild Indians plenty of trouble, so Kelly wasn't worried about her momentary safety. He was dog tired, having driven himself without mercy for the past three days. He took his horse to the livery, ordered first class care for it, then went to the

25

town's one hotel. He soon found himself in a hot bedroom on the second floor.

He stretched out on the ragged bed hoping to catch some sleep, but it wouldn't come. He could feel the metallic tautness of every nerve, the flat stupidity of his mind, the spent after-effects of the emotions that had run in him so long. Deep in this welter was a needling irritation. The thing was going to drag out, with himself obligated to remain on hand as a witness or else accept the risk of having to come the long way back from the Pecos. Waiting just wasn't his long suit.

He had managed to achieve a half slumber when somebody destroyed it by laying summary knuckles on the door. He stirred with a scowl, rose and walked in stocking feet to open up. The man who stood in the hall's bad light wore a hat on the back of his head. The deputy's badge on his vest glimmered faintly. Kelly felt the grain of his nerves reverse.

"Well, Rio," he drawled, "the last time I seen you, you were border jumping down south. How come you're packing that piece of tin?"

Rio Bell came on into the room. Kelly closed the door, nibbling his lip, wondering what was going to come of this. Bell stopped in the center of the room, hooked his thumbs in his belt. His cheeks showed a stain from that greeting.

"What're you doing here, Drake?" he asked.

"Good question for you, too. I was about to get some sleep when you butted in."

"All right," Bell said bitterly, "where's Jim Oliphant?"

"I dunno." Kelly grinned at him. "Does that mean Missus Jim's here in town with you? Didn't know you could stick to a woman that long, Rio."

26

"Answer me, damn it," Bell spat. "You didn't just happen to drift to this town. You and Jim always teamed up. You wouldn't come off out here without a reason. Likely not without him."

"Nor would he want another man to kill his snakes," Kelly agreed. His eyes goaded the man and had every cause. He'd stood up with Jim and Linda. He'd walked the floor with Jim when their baby was born. He'd trusted her the same as Jim had—too long.

Bell's own eyes glittered in their temper, but they showed a real concern beneath. That surprised Kelly. Physically this man had no fear. A strapping, muscular fellow with a smooth brown skin and glistening black hair, he could pick his women and laugh at the men whose rights he violated, then maybe beat them half to death or cripple or kill them with that gun on his hip. Yet he was afraid now, really afraid, and that fear had brought him to this room in record time.

"Look," Bell said desperately, "I've made a plumb fresh start. Mebbe I played fast and loose with the law once, but here I'm trying to make amends by workin' for it. I got a good reputation. A home here. And you could cost me my job with Charlic Redd, as well as ruin everything for Linda."

"Which do you dread the worst, Rio?"

"I know how you feel about me. But you grew up with her, the same as Jim did. Think of her."

"Neither one of you thought of Jim when she hit the trail with you."

Bell threw up his hands in frustration. "There's the boy."

"Jim's. Born in wedlock. Any more now, born otherwise?"

Renewed hostility flooded Bell's cheeks, and he was

done with begging. "I hoped you'd be reasonable, Drake," he said stiffly. "Since you ain't so inclined, let me lay it on the line in a way you'll understand. As far as you and Jim go, I'm ready for either one or both. What me and Linda done was wrong, and I don't deny it. But we've built a new life up here, and I won't let anything spoil it. I'm telling you."

"Simmer down, man. I had a hint you two were in this country. Then forgot it entirely till I seen you again in the sheriff's office. I admit it give me a turn."

"But why're you here, then?"

"You know a Chance Comber?" Kelly asked.

Bell gave him a quick, sharp look. "Sure. He runs the Horse Track. That's the biggest cow outfit in this valley."

"Well, he hired an Ogallala tart to slip me a micky," Kelly said. "I figured to settle that with him. Then I run into some of his dirty work out in the sand hills. That's all. I'd like to gut shoot you, Rio. But you're right about me not hankering to hurt Linda and the baby. I don't think it's in you to go straight. But, as long as you seem to be doing so, it's all right with me for you to pack that deputy's badge."

"But where's Oliphant?" Bell insisted.

"I tell you, I don't know."

Bell was a little relieved, though patently not much. Kelly resisted the impulse to taunt him with the fact that Jim knew exactly where to find his faithless wife and her lover. In strict fact, he didn't know where his saddlemate was and had a wonder about it, himself. It would be dangerous to Jim to warn Bell he might be lurking near right now, letting Bell get set.

"All right," Bell said. "For now that lays the chunk."

He left without farewell.

28

There was a dirty taste in Kelly's mouth afterward, and he had no further desire for sleep. He stood staring at the window, past which he could see the hot, unstirred leaves of a cottonwood tree. The softening atmosphere told him that evening had come. Restlessness more than hunger decided him to go out and get a meal. He tugged on his boots, the grim light in his eyes staying there, and he put on his hat and went out.

Building shadows now fell across the street, darkening it without bringing any coolness. Tramping along the board walk, he began to grow aware of the numbers of horses standing at the hitching racks wearing a double C burn. That was apt to be the brand of Chance Comber, he reflected—Bell had called the outfit Horse Track.

Kelly didn't know how close the spread was, or how frequently this many riders got into town. But at present the sidewalks were all but empty, the horses' owners being somewhere indoors. He turned into the first restaurant he came to.

He ate a steak half buried in stale fried potatoes and topped it off with a slab of dried peach pie. The coffee was such as to eat holes in a man's cheeks but he downed it. When it failed to take the flatness out of him, he decided it was time he had a drink.

He stepped onto the walk just as Charlie Redd swung past. The sheriff turned with a look of recognition, saying, "I was heading up to the hotel to see you, Drake," He flung a quick, uneasy glance along the street, then lowered his voice. "You better light your shuck, man. I don't like the looks of so many Horse Track punchers in town. I got a call I got to go out on, taking Rio with me. Could be a trick to get me outta here, or mebbe it's the real thing. But I got to go."

"Meanin'?"

"You're the main chance of swingin' the varmints that done away with Terry Kilrain. You better slip out of here and put up at the Running Iron. That's what they've taken to calling Badger Gamble's outfit, and he adopted it, himself. That's the safest place till I need you again."

Kelly grinned at him. "Thanks, but I can take care of myself."

"Lot of Horse Trackers in town, man. I don't like it."

The peace officer walked on.

Kelly stared after him a moment, feeling more of the worry that disturbed Redd than he had let show. But a rising anger was drowning that out. Chance Comber had won a trick from him and wasn't going to take another. Nor was Kelly Drake going to run from him or any man.

He saw up the street the sign of a saloon that called itself the Longhorn. There were more Horse Track cayuses posted at its rack than anywhere else on the long thoroughfare. Kelly moved up to its door and went in. He looked easy, but for the moment his tongue was glued to the roof of his mouth.

He entered the place so quietly he was half down the length of the bar before anybody noticed him. A man turning from the bar gave him a quick second look and sucked in his breath. Others turned and along the tables men looked up. From the cornermost group, Chance Comber sent Kelly a long, hostile stare.

There were three men seated there with Comber, strangers to Kelly but obviously from friendly big ranches or Horse Track's own payroll. Kelly moved with easy insolence as he crossed to their table.

"What's the matter, Comber?" he drawled. "Didn't you figure on that U.P. freight straying way off up here?"

"So," said Comber in a slow, dull way, "you're the son of a bitch that's chipped in with the nesters."

The insult was deliberate. The men with Comber were alert, tense in their chars. This hangout probably belonged to the big outfits, and Kelly could sense the belligerence at his back. Yet a crowding defiance carried him on.

"As one son of a bitch to another," he murmured, "you're dead right."

Shock jarred the features of Chance Comber. He'd applied the insult willingly enough, but now he'd got it back not only in front of his punchers but other men whose respect he dared not lose. The hostility in the men about the green-topped table bulged out at Kelly. They'd been seeking an excuse to pick a quarrel. It had come so swiftly they were all caught flat-footed. Now they searched for a way to handle it.

Comber was the coolest of them, showing nervousness only at the corners of his mouth. He looked around the table, at the men who stared at him and waited so intently with shuttling, stormy eyes. They all left it up to him. There was no way he could backtrack now.

"You got me at a disadvantage, Drake," the cowman said.

"Then stand up."

"I ain't armed."

The men listening did a fair job of concealing their surprise. Kelly shrugged and started to turn, and that did the trick. As he whirled back, he saw Comber shoving to a stand, his hand clawing up his gun. He hadn't

31

cleared leather with it when the sixgun that flashed into Kelly's fist spat its fire. Comber let go the gun grips, shaking a stung hand, incredulity twisting his face out of shape. The ruined pistol fell with a clatter to the floor.

By then Kelly had reached the side wall and pressed the flats of his shoulders against it.

"Easy, boys!" he warned the score of men who stood poised on the balls of their feet and fought the wild impulses in their gun hands. He began to edge along the wall toward the batwings.

They watched him steadily, the reputation he had not wanted having its effect on them. Comber, still working his fingers, was making some kind of growling sound in his throat. But nobody wanted to be the first to start trading lead. Kelly reached the batwings and backed through.

CHAPTER 4

ONCE KELLY WAS ON THE SIDEWALK HE BLEW OUT HIS cheeks. He had made the biggest fool play of his life and knew it already. Making a monkey out of Chance Comber had settled the Ogallala score. But it hadn't made this Lone Point town any safer for Kelly Drake. He might better have listened to Charlie Redd's advice.

He hurried along a street that was now night-shadowed. The lobby of the hotel was deserted when he hurried through. His room was at the back of the upper floor. He turned the handle of the door quickly and stepped in only when the door had completed its swing to bang against the wall.

"It's all right, Kelly," a voice said. "Only me."

He dimly saw her then, in the darkness, sitting on the

edge of the lumpy bed. He shut the door hastily, fished out a match and thumbed it ablaze. When he had lighted the oil lamp on the stand table, he turned to look at the girl.

"No reason for you to come here, Linda," he said coldly. "I told Rio all I had to say."

"He doesn't know about this. He had to go out of town with Charlie Redd."

Linda Oliphant, or whatever she called herself, was a slender woman with an exotic beauty, and her hair was the color of burnished copper. Her eyes, which had been deep pools of mystery to him back when he had known her very well, were a little harder, he thought. Once they had held warmth and a levelness that he'd liked. Now they disturbed him deeply. She was better dressed than she used to be when she and Jim were on their little ranch.

"I still don't know where Jim is," he said flatly. His gaze flicked her, and he didn't care if it had something of the effect of a whip.

"I never believed that, and neither did Rio."

"All right, he's on your trail," Kelly said angrily. "And what are you going to do about it—help Rio murder him?"

He saw a visible flinch at that. "You won't believe this, but I want to see him. I want to give Jimmy back to him."

"You would?" Kelly gasped.

"Tell Jim that if you know how to get in touch with him."

"So now you'd use your own child as a bribe."

Linda's cheeks sagged visibly. "Believe what you want about that. But I had another reason for coming here. You're in more danger than you seem to realize. You've got to get out of this town right now."

"I already had a brush with Comber. He didn't make the grade."

"You killed him?" What looked like hope shone for a moment in Linda's eyes.

"Just turned down his wick. Linda, why do you care about me?"

She looked away. "A person doesn't erase his memories, even when he loses his head. We grew up together, that's all. You're in trouble, Kelly, and I want to help you get out of town."

"As a matter of fact, I'd already decided to do just that."

"Don't try to get your horse. I'll get mine and bring it around back of the hotel. I can do it, all right. Please, Kelly. Trust me that far."

"So," he said softly, "the big love didn't last."

She looked up sharply. "I didn't say that."

"Not outright."

"Just let me help you, Kelly," she said, "and forget about me. Except to arrange for me to meet Jim in secret and turn Jimmy over to him."

He had a sudden ghastly insight into what her life must have been since she had cleared out with Rio and once the infatuation had collided with reality. But she wasn't whining, and somehow he believed that she did want to help him, to make what amends she could.

"How long do you need?" he asked.

"Give me ten minutes, and come out the back way. I'll be there."

She rose, and he saw the slim, unchanged suppleness of her lovely body. That sight brought back many things from the days when he had known her well. But she had been Jim's girl, and he had never let himself respond

34

greatly to the appeal she had for every man. She slipped out, pulling the door shut behind her.

Kelly stood there a long moment. She had certainly changed the impression Rio had tried to give of their new life here. She could not possibly know of a danger to him unless Rio knew it—or was himself the danger.

She wasn't trying to buy Jim off with the offer to return his son. There were deeper reasons why she wanted their child placed in other hands.

Thereafter Kelly worked with the controlled rush that never left him for long. He'd brought with him to the hotel his roll and saddlebags, the sum total of his property other than his gun, saddle and horse. He got a box of shells from a saddle pocket and filled the few empty loops in his belt. He double-checked the Colt .45. He hung the saddlebags over his shoulder and, picking up the sling, he moved over and blew out the lamp. He waited a few more minutes in darkness before he went out, hoping the downstairs lobby was still empty.

No sound came from the town now, when he would have welcomed the casual racket of a normal evening. He moved quietly down the stairway into a lobby still empty, then turned toward the hotel's rear door.

Before he stepped out, he paused for a quick look backward. Then he moved out into the alley behind the hotel. There was no horse there, and he pressed back against the wall, listening with distrustful care. Then he saw a mounted figure turn into the end of the alley. His ears picked up the soft sound of something more.

In the next second he swung, flinging the heavy roll in his hand. A man had stepped quietly from the shadows, and he had a gun. He apparently had meant to take a prisoner, but the roll, heavy with Kelly's kit, threw him back. Kelly jerked up his gun. The other gun

35

blazed first. The last thing he remembered thinking was: And I let another woman pull me into a trap . . .

Time and again, after that, he all but returned to consciousness only to have it move away from him again. Yet each time he nearly regained his senses, he received impressions he tried to put together in a way that meant something. Finally he was convinced that he was roped on a horse, and on the tail of that awareness came another. He was going wherever Terry Kilrain had gone. He was about to solve that mystery the hard way and so as to do no one but his enemies any good.

Pretty soon he could feel the saddle he forked and knew he was bent forward so that his roaring head bounced painfully with the up and down swing of the horse's neck. He was tied there, he found as he strained with his arms and legs. He still couldn't get his eyelids pulled apart. He didn't have to see. Whoever was riding ahead of him was picking the way, leading this horse. They were going pretty fast, which was why the jarring hurt him the way it did. Then it all slipped away from him again.

When next he opened his eyes, he realized that he lay in a bed somewhere, that daylight brightened the room. He remembered that horseback ride and wondered why Chance Comber would bother to put him to bed this way. He'd figured that by this time he'd be three feet under ground, Then bitterly he remembered Linda Oliphant and the treacherous trick he'd let her play on him. He had even more in common with Jim now. They both had tasted of her disloyalty.

He realized suddenly that the walls of this room were plastered with earth, that the floor was earthen, too. Although it was plain to the point of shabbiness, the small space was clean and very neat. That meant a

36

soddy somewhere, and he doubted that Comber would stoop to live in one. He grew extremely puzzled as he laid there, aware again of the roaring pain in his head. Then he drifted off to sleep.

When he awakened again, his head was completely clear. He realized that it was somebody's coming into the room that had aroused him. Yet his brain blurred with a moment's bewilderment when he saw the girl who stood in the doorway looking at him. She was motionless, as if she had tried to come in for something without disturbing him and now was aghast that she had.

"Abbie," he said. "How did I get here? As a matter of fact, where is here?"

She still wore calico, and her dark hair was curlier now than he remembered, like she had been fixing herself up. He noticed now that her nose had a tip at the end which turned upward a cute trifle. Her brows were arched full and high, and when she came on in he saw the slender legs again below her shrunken skirt.

"First," she said, "you're back where you started. It doesn't take long to fix up a soddy. The boys had this pretty well in shape before you showed up again."

"You're living on your own place?" he demanded. "Alone?"

"You've been here most of the time."

"But how did I get here?"

"Linda Bell brought you out."

"Linda Bell?"

He'd raised up a little, but he dropped back. Somehow he'd been wrong about Linda, and he wasn't going to set anybody here straight as to her real name.

"I understand you got yourself into quite a mess there," Abbie resumed. "She had to shoot a man to get you away."

37

Kelly closed his eyes, suppressing a groan. What had that done to her situation there in Lone Point? Rio Bell clearly was privy to knowledge about Comber's plans that had not been available to Charlie Redd. She'd known that a trap was being set for him, even before he'd gone into the Longhorn on that mad impulse, for she'd been waiting for him in his hotel room right afterward. He'd grown doubly convinced that Rio was playing a two-sided game with the law he professed to serve. Whatever, Kelly felt as beholden to Linda now as he was worried about her.

"When was that?" he gasped.

"Last night. You were creased by the bullet and a little more. Badger said you had a slight concussion, which couldn't hurt a Texan very bad."

"He been over here?"

She nodded. "He wants to talk to you as soon as you're able."

Kelly rubbed the stubble on his face and discovered the bandage on his head. "Able now." He raised up again but, with a groan, fell back. The movement had started a roar in his head and the room whirled about him. Weakly, he added, "Almost."

"You need something to eat. I've got some beef soup on the stove."

The very thought of eating was nauseating at the moment. But he knew he had lost a lot of strength. He nodded a reluctant agreement to her suggestion.

She was gone only a moment, and when she came back she brought a bowl of beef soup into which she had broken chunks of bread. The smell repelled him, but once he'd tasted the soup appetite came up fast. He ate it all.

"Want more?" she asked.

He shook his head. "I don't like the notion of you being here alone. A knocked-out man isn't much help any way you look at it."

"One of Badger's men has been staying here."

"That's better. Any news from Charlie Redd?"

The gravity of her face deepened noticeably, "Yes, there's news. He's dead. Homer Pritchard brought out the word just a while ago."

Headache or no, Kelly sat up in the bed at that. "What? How'd that happen?" The sickness was back in his mouth, turning him weak.

"He and Rio Bell were called out of town. Apparently into a gun trap. Somebody dry-gulched them out east of Turkey Creek. Shot Charlie out of the saddle. Rio fought back, but they got away from him. They buried Charlie today."

"And who'll be the new sheriff?" Kelly asked harshly.

"The county officials have already appointed Rio."

The illness of his mouth and throat went all through Kelly. For a moment he had to close his eyes. When he opened them again, Abbie was staring at him worriedly.

"I might of saved Charlie," he groaned. "But I never dreamed it went that deep. Charlie suspected it was a trick, but to get him out of town so they could get at me. Abbie, Rio knew what was going to happen to Charlie Redd when they left. I'll bet he shot Charlie in the back and made up his dry-gulching yarn."

"What on earth are you talking about?" she asked and sounded scared.

"I knew Rio down south. He was smuggling across the border and mixing up in any other dirty business that would turn him a dollar. You acted suspicious of him yourself, the other day when you asked him to leave before you talked to Charlie."

Abbie nodded. "We've known all along he was nowhere near as impartial as Charlie."

"He's pocketing Comber money. And I've got to tell the county officers the truth."

Bitterness rose on her face. "That wouldn't do any good. They're all big ranchers. Charlie wouldn't take their orders and—"

"And," Kelly concluded for her, "now they've got a sheriff who will. Comber's hands are freed, where he had to consider Charlie's brand of law before. Things will really hump from here on. I've got to see this Badger Gamble."

"He's coming over again this evening."

Abbie went out with the empty bowl. For a long while afterward Kelly lay there thinking: I doomed Charlie, anyhow speeded up his death. Rio had to kill him before I got Charlie suspicious enough to fire him. I wonder if Linda knew what was going to happen, too. Then, the soup strengthening and easing him physically, he grew drowsy and once more slept.

When he opened his eyes again, it was with the old sense of well-being. He realized from the changed atmosphere that another night must have passed, a morning come. His head ached a little when he stood up but soon quit. His clothes were neatly folded on a chair, the blood he had spilled on them washed away and the garments ironed. He dressed, feeling stronger by the minute, knowing he was going to need that strength.

He discovered when he stepped out that the bedroom he'd been using was the only one. The main room, surprisingly re-roofed with dirt and showing little signs of damage now, was used for all other living purposes,

40

and Abbie was asleep there on a rawhide cot. He carried his razor and he went on out. There was water in a bucket on the bench by the door, a small mirror pegged to the wall.

He filled the tin basin, washed up, then shaved. Removing the bandage, he found that the shallow wound on the crown of his head was scabbed over. He left the bandage off and figured from the mirror's reflection that he was back in business again. Abbie was still asleep when he went back inside.

Shoving back the curtain on a set of wall shelves, he saw all he needed to make their breakfast. The cooking was all done in the fireplace at the end of the room, and he made a fire. He put coffee on the hook above the flames and located a Dutch oven. He began to put together the makings of a batch of biscuits.

"Land of goodness!"

He turned. Abbie had sat up in bed, astonished. Then, under his stare, she grew aware that she wore only a nightgown and was displaying considerable of it. She flattened herself in confusion and pulled the blankets up to her chin. Her hair was tousled, and her breasts nicely lifted the covers.

"Kelly Drake, you've no business being up."

"Plenty," he retorted. "And your breakfast will be ready in a jiffy."

"Well, keep your back turned. I've got to go to the bedroom to dress."

"How about Badger's man? Don't he ever eat?"

"He's been sleeping in the stable."

"Badger here last night?"

"Yes. When he saw you were so dead to the world, he said he'd try again this morning."

She slipped into the bedroom while he went on with

41

his chores. He was glad she was the type not to grieve uselessly for her missing father. Life was hard for any frontier woman, harder even than it was for the men. Women had to come back fast from their tragedies, had to accept them and go on living. Nobody had any hope they'd ever find Terry Kilrain alive, and from there on the problems would be hers to meet.

When she came out in her shrunken dress and moccasins, her legs still bare and brown, he estimated that the top of her head would meet his chin. But she wasn't going to let it come that close, not with a ring-tailed Texan.

She surprised him by saying without preamble, "What do you look for in all your rambling?"

He stared, the sudden suspicion in him that she'd been reading his thoughts. "One thing and then another."

"Ever find it?"

"One way or another."

"A girl, I suppose," she murmured. "Or a fight."

"Both worth looking for," he said judiciously.

"But neither ever mean much, do they?"

He was stung by that. Roughly, he said, "Go wake up our chaperone. I've about got breakfast ready."

She went out. When she returned he saw she'd washed her face and combed her hair. A man she introduced simply as Colorado followed her, a blocky, wizen-faced fellow Kelly himself would never have appointed her guardian. Yet when the man grinned and gave a strong, warm handshake, Kelly changed his mind about that. They sat down to eat.

"Before I meet this Badger Gamble," Kelly said, "I'd like to know a little more about him."

"He's as fine a man as ever lived," Abbie replied.

"And that," said Colorado, "sums it up. Any man who ever hit these parts in trouble has found a friend in him."

"Or got into trouble after he came here," Abbie added. "Which would include me in."

"Badger seems to be quite impressed by you."

"Which you ain't."

"Which I am, but not quite in the same manner."

Looking at Colorado, Kelly said, "That Running Iron moniker sure sounds like a rustler's."

Colorado laughed. "That's what Badger is, if you want to look at his setup the way the big cow outfits do. So, according to their lights, is every other little coffeepot spread in the sand hills. But Badger claims he's only running a collection agency. And that's how a lot of others see it, too. You tell him, Abbie. The man makes pretty good biscuits, and I'm hungry."

"Well," Abbie said, "in the first place Comber and Badger used to be partners up on Powder River. Then they went broke. That is, Badger found out he'd gone broke while Comber hadn't."

"Sounds like Comber," Kelly agreed.

"He did the book work," Abbie said, "while it was Badger who built up their spread and made it pay. They failed, even so. Yet for some mysterious reason Comber had the money to set up a fine new spread in this country. Badger knew he'd been fooled and cheated but couldn't do a thing. So he set up next door to Horse Track and started rustling back what he'd lost. When the big spreads started calling his little place the Running Iron, he adopted it with pleasure. Yet not a one of them has ever been able to pin a thing on Badger. Which is gall and wormwood to Chance Comber."

"I swear," said Colorado, his mouth momentarily

43

empty, "he gets so much fun out of it, he don't care if he ever collects all he's got coming or don't."

"How about the other nesters that have thrown in with him?" Kelly asked.

"One way or another," Colorado told him, "they've all got a case of some kind against Horse Track or Childress' Zigzag or Clyde Murchison's M Bar. Some're cowboys that have been abused, misused, double-crossed or rooked. Others got busted on sharp cattle deals. Terry Kilrain invested money in Horse Track before he come out here and learned about Comber's fast book work. When he thinks about it all, Badger gets real serious and aims to collect in full plus a reasonable interest."

"Why'd they move against Kilrain first?" Kelly wondered.

"Badger better explain that to you. It ties in with the way they've all homesteaded across a good piece of Comber's range. What he likes to call his, that is. Actually, it was all done through honest entries." Colorado grinned. "You got a case against Horse Track yet?"

"I reckon I have."

"Then," said Colorado, "you're one of us."

CHAPTER 5

BADGER GAMBLE WORE A GREASY BLACK HAT ATOP A gray and patently rambunctious head. His seamy brown face held humor and the stubbornness of a freighter's mule, while his voice had the crack of the skinner's whip. He swung down in front of the soddy before those within had finished breakfast and walked in.

44

"Morning, Badger," Abbie greeted, and Colorado tipped his boss an easy nod.

"Howdy," said Badger, hardly seeing them for Kelly Drake who seemed to occupy his full attention. "So you're the bugger that's been tying knots in the tail of old Chance Comber."

"Infringing on your rights?" Kelly said and grinned.

He shook the rancher's hand, surprised at the tallness of the man. Badger Gamble looked thin but, just the same, he probably added up to a lot of pounds.

"Plenty of room for company," Badger answered. "And if you're feeling good enough this morning, you can ride to town with me. I aim to lay down a little law to our new sheriff."

Kelly switched his sudden stare from the man to Abbie. "Did you tell him I know a chapter or so of Rio Bell's life?"

"Last night while you were sawing wood," Badger answered for her. "Although I doubt that will help much. What you say and what you can prove are horses of two different shades."

"The county officers crooks?"

"I wouldn't say that. But they ain't ever wept over us nesters and worked to improve our lot in life. They'd rather not believe you, unless you forced proof down their throats. Which I don't reckon you're fixed to do."

"Then what good can he do in town?" Abbie asked. She looked worried about such a visit.

"Mainly," said Badger, "I want a long talk with Kelly and ain't got the time to roundside here doing it."

"Be right with you," Kelly said.

He'd about given up hope of somehow amputating Rio Bell from his new job. But he was still worried about Linda and what she might have suffered from

45

helping him out of Chance Comber's trap. He also kept wondering about Jim, experiencing a half-sick dread of his showing up in Lone Point alone and uninformed of present circumstances. On top of that, his own horse and saddle were still in the stable in town.

Linda, he learned when he visited the corral with Colorado, had ridden her own horse back to town. Kelly grinned when he saw the Horse Track mount in Abbie's corral, which Linda had been forced to grab off the street to transport him, Colorado explained. Kelly remembered that she'd been obliged to shoot the man who'd plugged him, as well. With the town on edge the way it had been, she must have worked fast and furious. She couldn't possibly have done it in secret.

"That will be a touchy cayuse to ride to town," Kelly commented.

"You can take one of Abbie's."

"Not me. When I borrow a cayuse, I take it back where I got it."

"You're the type of huckleberry," Colorado said, "that dies happy but real young."

Kelly was soon riding out on the town trail with Badger Gamble. The morning was already brassy hot. Moved by the prairie wind, the air here and there was filled with dust. Badger was silent, almost grumpy for a time. He had Kelly curious, but the younger man didn't crowd the talk.

"I hear," Badger said finally, "that you're a gadding kind of man."

"You didn't hear anything very good about me from Abbie."

"Not much," Badger admitted. "She don't figure a woman ought to hitch her wagon to a shooting star."

"I ain't proposed to her."

Badger grinned. "First thing any woman does when she sees a new man is size him up as husband material. All but the right one she shoves in with the throwbacks. That tended to, she's ready for other business. Which is what I better get down to."

"Have at it."

"I been wondering if you might be interested in sojournin' with us a spell. This country's got deviltry enough for any man, includin' Texans, with some left over for the women. I'm satisfied and, me, I started out like you, plumb itchy-footed."

"I hear," Kelly said, not wanting to answer Badger's question, "that you once went pardners with Chance Comber."

"In a period of extra lunacy, the way it turned out. I gave the cuss his start. It was a maverickin' start, too, the same as most of the other big outfits got. Neither one of us had a window to throw it out of when we set up in business. Colorado remembers."

"He been with you a long time?" Kelly asked.

"He was my ramrod then and still is. I got a place for a man of your cut, too, if you don't mind getting killed." Badger was rolling himself a smoke, having no trouble with the wind. He licked the paper and hung the cigarette on his long lip. "How about it?"

Kelly shook his head. "Me, I got my settling down over when I was real young. But I might listen to something of a temporary nature."

"Me," Badger said, "I've done more studyin' of the land office maps than the commissioner, himself. Stumbled onto something a while back. Wasn't looking for it, but when it sneaked up and bit me, I knowed I had the tail hold on old Chance I been hunting for years."

47

"That sure don't sound like a lasting job."

Badger laughed. "It sure wouldn't be once that old grabber caught on. I'm trusting you with information only Colorado shares with me. Chance's got a main winter line camp he don't own. But he don't realize that yet. I'd like to get somebody to homestead it before he starts to use it this fall. Somebody, that is, on our side of the set-to. You ever used your homestead rights?"

"No. But how come Comber would be so careless?"

"He don't realize he has been," Badger said. "It's in the boundary line description. Must have looked at that line a dozen times, myself, before I tumbled, and I kind of specialize in finding Horse Track weaknesses. The line's about a hundred yards farther north than everybody always figured. Which puts Comber's camp and the water hole for that whole piece of range on a vacant quarter just south. One I had my eye on at the time I made the find."

"He couldn't get any other water around there?"

"Not without drilling some wells or runnin' the fat off his steers as fast as they could put it on. We checked the thing out real careful, on the sly. That government survey last year altered things some. Enough to put a cocklebur under that old snort hog's tail."

"Likewise under the gent's who set himself up on such a claim."

"You're right there," Badger admitted. "But I aimed to homestead the empty piece, anyhow. The rest, when I checked it out, come as a pure bonus. The claim is just north of Abbie's. We been edging too close to that camp already to suit Chance. That's why he done away with Terry Kilrain the first."

"And whoever goes on the new claim will stand between her and Horse Track."

"As long as he sticks there. You like her well enough to do it?"

"I like her plenty. But no woman is any good to a dead man."

"Thought I'd mention it," Badger said.

The trail joined the road in from the railroad, presently. Swiftly the rounded sand hills fell behind, the big valley of the Standing Rock opening up. Finally Badger pointed north.

"That ex-Horse Track line camp's up that way."

"Ex, is it?"

"One way or another, it's ex."

They reached Lone Point around noon, which had a quieter look than on the day of Kelly's first visit. Now it lay flat and hot and sleepy under the hot fall sky. He took a look at the northward country, this time, knowing the big cattle outfits were up there, occupying the whole of the valley. The nester colony was in the sand hills at the eastern edge but pressing hard on the valley now, meaning, as Badger had just intimated, to move into it at last.

Kelly's sympathies for the nesters were not lessened by the fact that they were on the aggressive, as Chance Comber had complained so bitterly in Ogallala. Actually, according to Colorado and Abbie, they only sought redress for past losses and injuries. The courts could not do that for them because of Comber's cleverness or else would not because of the strong political power of the big stockmen.

Kelly left Badger at the edge of town, feeling it would do no good to see Rio Bell in the man's company, since what lay between them personally was a much more private matter than Badger's business. He'd about decided not to return with the nester leader, instead remaining here to play out his private string.

49

As they separated, Badger eyed Kelly a moment. "Don't let 'em have another crack at you," he warned.

"I'm no good as a witness in the Kilrain case any more," Kelly replied. "Mainly because the new sheriff'll see that there ain't ever any such case."

"You're probably dead right."

Kelly was both restless and uncertain as he let Badger ride on toward the courthouse. It was not anxiety over the obvious danger that still lay for him in this country. Nor was it anything he could put his finger on accurately. He was aware that be wanted to locate Jim Oliphant, if Jim had actually headed for these parts. He wanted to find Linda and express his gratitude and see if he couldn't help her in return. Yet these things failed to explain all the bewildering disturbances in him. Maybe it was Badger's proposition that had upset him, or his own refusal of it.

He rode the Horse Track horse to the livery and turned it over to a surprised hostler, telling the man to take care of it and send it home by the first Comber rider he saw. But he didn't ask for his own mount immediately. He took himself to the hotel he had stayed at previously and registered for another room.

It was no better than the first one, and he took it only because he knew he might have to wait a while for a chance to see Linda or to encounter Jim. He didn't like the prospect of a long, idle interim but saw no way around it. In the room he washed off the trail dust and brushed it from his clothes. But he only felt more restless and at loose ends.

He managed to remain in the room, at the window where he could watch the street, for only about an hour. Descending the stairs, he halted at the desk. A wispy clerk without any teeth looked up at him.

"Where does Rio Bell live?" Kelly asked.

"The new sheriff? You'd find him at the courthouse this time of day. If he's in town."

"Thanks," Kelly said. He'd hoped the man would answer the question directly instead of trying to be so helpful. But it wouldn't be smart to press, and he could find out some other way. He went on to the street.

He had his noon meal. The town was still peaceful, not nearly as stirred up by his arrival as he'd expected. Badger's horse was still tied in front of the courthouse. Some punchers in bow-legged Levis loafed on the sidewalk, paying him no notice. It looked like he could relax a little, and he wanted a drink. He went into the Longhorn saloon.

At this hour only the bar was being given any use, and that not much. The few men there showed a complete indifference to his presence. Kelly had a drink, then bought a bottle and took it back to his hotel room. Again he sat down at the window for a long, watchful wait.

The only thing he'd seen an hour later was Badger coming along the street, probably looking for him. Kelly whistled through the open window, caught the man's attention and motioned to him to come up.

Badger had a look of surprise on his face when he stepped into the room. "How come?" he asked.

"Reckon I'll hang around a while," Kelly answered. "Have a drink."

"As a social gesture," Badger agreed, "and also because I'm dry. It's none of my never-mind what you do here, bub, but if I was you I wouldn't hang one on just now."

"Don't aim to. There's some private things, Badger, and then I don't know what. But I'll be out to thank

51

everybody and say goodbye before I pull stakes, if I do."

Badger took a long pull on the bottle. "So you might roll your tail?"

"I ain't decided. But you haven't drove your spikes through my feet, if that's what you mean."

"Mebbe I never," Badger admitted. "But I'm still hoping somebody else did."

"Abbie? She don't like it up here with us shootin' stars. You said so, yourself."

"A woman don't have to like a man to hammer in her nails."

"Have another drink."

"Thanks," said Badger and did.

"You see Rio?"

Badger wiped his mouth with the back of his hand. "It's what we figured. He ain't interested in the case of Terry Kilrain no more. He's plumb tied up, he says, finding out who bushwhacked his closest friend and idol, Charlie Redd."

"What's he going to do when he catches up with himself?"

"That," said Badger, "is a question I could ask you. What'll you do when you do?"

The tall man left then, not showing any special disappointment that Kelly had turned his proposal down. Kelly sat chewing on that parting remark for a long while. Once Jim Oliphant, a much steadier man, had accused him of chasing his own tail. Well, maybe that was what he had been doing.

He had another long pull on the bottle, then wiped off the sweat distilled on his forehead by the afternoon's mounting heat. Pretty soon he realized that, without much help from Badger, the whiskey was half gone. He batted his eyes sleepily, then went over to the bed and stretched out.

He awakened with a throbbing ache in his temples, his throat feeling like an alkali sink. But his senses were clear again. Moving back to the window, he seated himself on the chair and rolled a cigarette. Then it was that he saw Rio Bell riding down the street, heading north, out of town.

A lively light leaped into Kelly's eyes. He'd lay two to one that Rio was going out to Horse Track and talk over Badger's visit, and whatever had been said between them, with Chance Comber. That didn't matter. The day was wearing out, and this could give him his chance to see Linda. He permitted himself one more drink to take the raw edge off his nerves.

He went down to the street level, emerging onto the board walk. The last hot sun had disappeared behind the westside buildings. He moved down to the batwings of the Longhorn. He wanted to ask a question. The courthouse would be closed by now, which gave him a good excuse for asking how to find Rio's residence.

Then, as he entered the saloon, he found himself staring down the bar at Trench Durnbo, Smiley Dennis and Pete Koster, the latter with his arm in a sling. They were watching the door in the back-bar mirror, as men of their breed did, and they all swung about to face Kelly, wary instantly.

Their open appearance here confirmed every suspicion Kelly had entertained about Rio's secret tie-in with Comber. They knew they had no need to fear the law, now, in Lone Point. Anger exploded in Kelly's brain at their insolence, at this plain evidence of the deep change for the worse in the country. Yet this was

53

not the time to pick a quarrel. He had to go easy unless they crowded him.

Yet it robbed him of his chance to ask directions of the bartender. But he'd entered the place and couldn't leave, especially under these circumstances. He could see the lively interest in the faces of the three men who watched him walk over to the bar. The men already gathering at the tables for the evening were aware of it, too. The thing had to be accepted, Kelly knew. He ordered whiskey.

The hardcase trio turned back to their own drinks but still watched the back mirror closely. Kelly took his time with his own liquor, not showing a hint of haste. It dawned on him slowly that they were not going to crowd him, and then he saw why. They'd heard what he'd done to Comber's gun in this same saloon.

They weren't so drunk yet that they were ready to try their own luck against his speed and accuracy. Kelly paid for the drink and walked out.

CHAPTER 6

THE BUTTON WHO SCUFFED OUT OF THE MERCANTILE wore oversize boots and carried a pail of lard. Kelly stopped him at the corner with a friendly grin.

"Pardner, where'd a man find the new sheriff this time of day?"

"Ain't he at the courthouse?"

"Locked tighter than a bull's eyes in fly time. Where's he live?"

The youngster turned and pointed. "You go up past Carmichael's saddlery and then turn right. The last house up that path is Bell's."

54

"Thanks. You like jawbreakers?" Kelly tossed the grinning kid a quarter. "Go back and lay in a supply."

Night was closing in fast now. But Kelly had no intention of going openly to Linda's house since he'd probably given her a lot of trouble already. When the youngster had vanished back into the store to buy his candy, Kelly turned in the other direction. He walked on to the end of the street, seeming to seek no more than exercise.

Rolling a cigarette, he observed that there was a back road so poor it showed little recent use. Past it was the brush of the creek bank. He sauntered on over to the stream and there seated himself to have his smoke.

He waited there until the night was full and lamplight showed in the windows. Then he rose, feeling the lifting beat of his heart, and moved along the creek bank, hidden to the town by the growth. When he came to a footbridge he halted and turned left along the trail leading back into the settlement. Coming out of the brush, he saw the back of a house. There was a girl on the rear porch, and the girl was Linda, he saw by the light of the open door behind her. She put something down, turned and went back indoors.

He moved quietly to the porch, making sure nobody was watching. He knew he'd alarm her when he knocked at this particular door but had to do it.

When he heard her uneasy inquiry, he called, not loudly, "It's Kelly, Linda. I got to see you."

The door opened at once, and while he stared at her he knew what she had paid for helping him. There was a bruise at the edge of her eye and her lower lip was puffed. She caught his arm and drew him on in, hastily shutting the door.

"You shouldn't have come here!" she breathed. "And you can't stay!"

"I watched Rio leave town."

"He won't be back tonight, but—" Then her eyes widened. "Kelly, have you seen Jim?"

"No. I had to thank you for what you done for me. I see what it cost you and if you hadn't been the new sheriff's—uh, wife, I reckon you'd have been in even worse trouble."

The light in the room came full on her strained features. "It's over now."

"Just why," he said harshly, "should Rio resent you siding somebody marked for boot hill by Chance Comber? Or was it just your siding me?"

"I can't talk about it, Kelly."

"Nor can you keep me from realizing you've had a bellyful of this new life of yours. Let me help you, Linda. You shot a man for me and must of had to stand a few more off while you got me on a horse and away. I owe you plenty for that. I want to take you and the baby both away from here."

"Please, please go."

In a furious, shoving way he said, "You know Rio's up to something bigger and rottener than anything he ever pulled before. You don't have to help break it up, but you can get out of it."

Her hands raised in desperation and clenched into fists. "Don't crowd me, Kelly! I can't betray two men, one's enough! I'm not excusing myself. You and Jim both tried to tell me Rio is rotten. I couldn't believe that—until I found out for myself. I made my bed. I don't want any sympathy."

"I think Jim would take you back."

"No," she said brokenly. Then suddenly she looked at

56

him with quick, bright wonder. "Kelly, there *is* something you can do if you feel you've got to repay me. Take Jimmy to Jim for me. Please."

"Why? To keep Jim from bracing Rio?"

"That's part of it," Linda admitted. "Rio's a gunman, and Jim never was. But it's mostly the baby. I'm not a fit mother. This isn't the kind of a home he ought to have. If you'll take him and go where even I don't know where you are, I'll be grateful to you the rest of my life."

"You mean it, don't you?"

"I've never meant anything more."

Kelly gave that close, furious thought. He felt as she did about Jim's chances of surviving a gun fight with Rio Bell. He certainly agreed that little Jimmy Oliphant should not grow up under Rio's tutelage and care. And he knew that the mother was determined to make the best of the life she had chosen voluntarily.

Softly he said, "What would Rio do if Jimmy vanished?"

"He'd be suspicious, but it wouldn't matter. Otherwise, he hates Jimmy."

"All right," Kelly said promptly. "I'll do it, then. How soon'll Rio be back?"

"He expected to stay at Horse Track all night."

"I got to get my horse," he said. "And we better wait till most of the town's bedded down. You have Jimmy ready. I'll be at this back door around midnight."

"All—all right."

He left her at once, not wanting to watch the stricken look that faintly showed in her eyes, although she was determined to go through with the arrangement.

He got his own horse from the livery and paid the feed bill. Racking it in front of the hotel, he went into the lobby and asked for or a sheet of paper and an envelope. Going on up to his room, he seated himself at the stand table and, by the greasy lamplight, began to write with the stub of a lead pencil.

"Jim, don't stay in this town a minute. Go out to a nester ranch in the sand hills that calls itself the Running Iron. The baby'll be there or somewheres near. Linda wants you to have him. She done me a big favor, Jim, and I don't want her abused any more than she's been already. On top of that, Rio's looking for you to show up. He won't give you a chance if he can help it. I mean it, Jim."

He sealed the letter in the envelope and addressed it to Jim, knowing the man would come openly if he came at all. Descending the stairs, he handed the message to the clerk with a ten dollar bill.

"If a man of that name starts to register," he said, "you give him this right off."

"Sure," the man said and looked like he would.

Kelly figured he had some two or three hours to kill before going back to Linda's to get the baby. Mounting his horse, he left town by the northern road, riding openly. If Trench Durnbo or anybody else proposed to follow him, he wanted it settled before he had Jimmy Oliphant on his hands. The road topped a rise, and as he came up over it he saw ahead the first stand of timber he'd observed in this country. He kept on leisurely.

Reaction had taken the hard set from his shoulders, and he felt inert and spent. Again he was becoming involved in a perplexity that would not yield to his probing. Somehow he was no longer his own man, and that change had come involuntarily, inexorably, in just the past few days. What he had agreed to do for Linda would hold him here indefinitely, and depression was an added weight to the weariness of his frame.

When he had come abreast of the timber he swiveled in the saddle for a careful look at his backtrail. He could see nobody following him but the darkness of the night made it wholly unwise to assume that this was the fact. He left the road and moved into the timber, which he saw was a patch of dwarfed cedar trees. The silence was so profound that the breathing of his horse was loud to him.

He didn't penetrate the growth more than enough to conceal himself and the horse. Swinging down, he loosened the saddle cinch, trailed reins, and moved back to where he could keep a steady eye on the trail. The animal began to graze peacefully, but Kelly found his own restlessness only worsened by the job of waiting he could not avoid.

Within minutes a sudden attention in the horse swung him about. He still could see nothing on the backtrail but trusted the beast's sharper hearing and instinct for its own kind. Moving over, he stood where he could keep it from whickering.

In a minute he could hear the hit and break of hoofs on the trail. Three horsemen, riding at a trot, passed his hiding place. They were the ones he had expected, Durnbo, Dennis and Koster. They were going to beat a lot of empty country before they found out that they had already lost their little game.

Yet he did not leave his position until the wheeling stars told him the middle of the night had come. Tightening the latigo, then, he went up to leather and rode back toward Lone Point at a steady clip. He moved in toward the Standing Rock as he approached the town, thereafter moving through the brush of the stream.

The Bell house was wholly dark when he came up behind it, as were its neighbors. He left his horse in the concealment of the stream vegetation and went on slowly, carefully, afoot. Linda must have been waiting intently and heard his tread on the porch. The door opened immediately.

"Is that you, Kelly?"

"Yes."

Almost he hoped that she would back out. But she whispered, "He's ready. I made up a little bundle of his things. You better tie it on the saddle first."

She picked up something from a table just within the room and handed it to him. It was soft, a roll wrapped in what would be a baby's blanket. He couldn't look at her as he took it and turned away. And he didn't hurry about lashing it onto the cantle and going back.

She was a long while coming out again. When she did, she walked swiftly. Little Jimmy's size surprised Kelly although he remembered that by now the boy would be around three years old. Although he probably could walk, the mother carried him. She handed him swiftly to Kelly.

"Don't—don't move till I'm back inside," she whispered. She whirled and fled. He stared for a moment afterward at the door she had closed. He didn't know what she must have told the boy to make him accept this so quietly, but there was no sound from Jimmy. Then Kelly turned and started toward his waiting horse.

CHAPTER 7

DAWN WAS MAKING ITS WARM, BRIGHT CRAWL OVER the eastern hills when Kelly rode in to the little Kilrain spread. Jimmy Oliphant had slept most of the way but was awake now, by his own insistence forking the

60

saddle in front of Kelly. At the door of the soddy, Kelly lifted him and swung down. He nearly reeled from fatigue, steadied himself and walked to the door. He rapped, knowing Abbie would still be asleep.

"Me, Abbie," he called. "The bad penny returned."

She opened the door at once and then pulled straight, her sleepy mouth gaping open.

"Where on earth did you get that baby?"

"Baby?" Kelly inquired. "Jimmy, spit in her eye for that insult. He's a real cowpoke, but about the wiggliest one I ever tried to set a saddle with."

Abbie had a wrapper about her nightgown and was still amazed.

"If you're not going to get us some breakfast," Kelly said, "get out of the way and let us men do it."

He went on in and put Jimmy down on the bed Abbie had just vacated. His face sobering, he said, "Might as well tell you the whole story. His mother and dad are old friends of mine. I grew up with 'em. Then Linda lost her head over a man you know and run off with him. They come to Lone Point."

"You—you mean Linda Bell?"

"Her legal name's Oliphant. I thought she was a tramp till lately. She saved my life, and it cost her plenty to do it. But it cost her even more when she give me Jimmy to take back to his father. She don't expect to see him again, didn't know where I'd head. But Jim— that's his dad—was coming this way the last time I seen him. I left a note at the hotel he might get. If he does, he'll show up here. He loved this kid, and he loved its mother."

Abbie was looking at Jimmy, a mounting excitement in her eyes.

"You cute little dickens!" she breathed.

61

Jimmy was all of that. His tousled hair was coppery, like his mother's, his eyes very brown. There was a child's relaxed trust about him still, now with a lively interest in this new place. He rolled onto his stomach and expertly dropped himself to the floor. He got busy with his investigations.

"Was it all right to bring him here?" Kelly asked.

"All right? This Jim's going to have trouble taking him away again."

Somebody was coming toward the house. The door opened, and Colorado stood there. The homely puncher's features stiffened when be saw the youngster.

"God A'mighty!" he exploded. "Things kin sure move fast!"

"He ain't ours, Colorado," Kelly said, laughing. "He's just loaned for a spell." He had it all to explain again.

He saw at once that his nursemaid hours were over. Abbie spent half her time cooking breakfast, the rest playing with Jimmy. She opened the roll Linda had sent along and investigated his wardrobe.

"You can sleep with me," she promised.

"You young hound," Kelly accused Jimmy.

Abbie laughed.

Kelly ate his breakfast, realizing he had brought her the very thing she needed to keep her mind off her father, missing, undoubtedly murdered, with little chance now of justice ever being done. He figured he had earned his keep and went down to the barn to sleep.

When he awakened he was instantly restless, as he had been the day before in the hotel. He was not a man who liked to have events crowd him along a course of action. It would be better for his peace of mind, he knew, if he reached his decision voluntarily. He stepped out through the archway of the dugout stable, went at once to the corral.

He'd turned his own tired mount loose to rest and graze. But there was a little hay in the barn now, and he suspected Badger had sent it over after Abbie had been thrown on her own. There was a rested horse in the corral that Badger probably had insisted on her keeping up in case of a sudden need. He roped and saddled it.

Abbie had not noticed him, and he rode out, heading north. Crossing the first ridge, he saw for the first time the steers than ran in the Kilrain Winged K, not many of them but good-looking stock. Except for the grass on which they fed, there was little vegetation.

His horse followed some kind of trail, and since he had only a hazy idea of where he wanted to travel he let the trace lead him on. Occasionally other trails crossed this one, old as time, worn by Indians or buffalo and other game. Then finally he found himself upon a rim at the edge of what looked to be a main valley. He stood his horse there while absently he fished out makings and rolled a cigarette.

Below him ran what he knew to be the land Badger wanted to contest with Chance Comber. Close at hand was a patch of mixed cottonwood and willow, with two small buildings thrown in. That meant a water hole, a line camp. There was no other tree—the sign of water—between this rim and the one beyond, at a distance of maybe half a mile. Comber's winter pasture must run mainly to the east of here. Kelly saw at a glance it would be a combination of grass, shelter and water that any cowman would hate to lose.

He could see also what must have happened in regard to the tricky boundary line Badger figured to exploit. Anybody would take this rim to be the natural division.

In the old days, when men picked their quarter sections to suit themselves, that surely would have been it. But surveys had laid things out in ways that no longer agreed with local geography.

Measuring up from Abbie's line, using figures he'd got at the land office, Badger had been able to determine where this line actually lay. Comber either hadn't tumbled or else hoped nobody else ever would. The little strip of land, itself, amounted to nothing. But the water rose naturally at the base of the rim, and, since there was no other supply, that meant everything. Kelly knew of instances where men had been shot and killed over such disputes.

The claim that was still open to filing, he reflected, ran from somewhere past that line camp down to Abbie's line. Thus he was standing his horse on it now. It didn't matter to the scheme where the east and west boundaries ran. A fine, legitimate land claim was here and his for the taking. It surely looked worth having, and he meant to look at what would be its headquarters.

He swung back from the rim, found an easy descent and, not much later, rode into the little half-dugouts at the spring. There was a good flow there, and he watered his horse. Excitement rose, and he could feel nerves and muscles easing in him. He kept watching that he wasn't discovered by a Horse Track rider.

The walls of the little house, and again of the diminutive stable, were made of cottonwood logs from the stand that ran out along the seep. But they were only half walls, raised around dugout holes under pole and dirt roofs. There were a couple of small corrals attached to the stable. A Horse Track cowpoke probably wintered here every year. But, he saw with a kind of possessive inspection, the place needed plenty of repair work.

He stepped down to the door of the house and found that it wasn't locked. He saw that it was kept stocked with food for the occasional summer use of Horse Track riders. He had a notion to have a meal on Chance Comber, then decided against it. There was a cookstove, a pair of bunks tacked to the wall, a table and two rough chairs. He sat down in one to scratch his jaw, then roll and smoke another cigarette.

He was mighty tempted, and the thing ran deeper than a chance to tweak Comber's hawk's nose. The big cattle outfits had their own county machinery now, their own law. They had struck two hard blows in the few days he had been in the country, in the murders of Kilrain and Redd. They were set to crowd it harder now, even more carelessly and callously, having nothing to fear except from the nesters themselves.

It was surely past time Comber was rocked back hard on his heels. Badger's scheme would throw him off stride, upset his schedule, and force him to new and unwelcome efforts. Something of that nature had to be done now; there was no mistaking that. Any way he looked at it, Kelly saw a duty he could not blink away and forget.

Sticking on this claim, if he filed, would be anything but easy, he knew well. He would have every big outfit in the Standing Rock to buck. But also he would have the whole nester colony behind him. If he lived long enough, he might have Comber yelling uncle, for no cowman ever had winter range to spare. Too much cramping could be disastrous.

"You like Abbie that much?" Badger had asked.

Kelly was sure that he did. He was eased at last, and

his mind was made up. He had been at loose ends too long. That was what had been working on him so annoyingly. It also was what Abbie did not like about him, a quality of which even Badger disapproved. Well, he would have to see old Badger pronto and find out where and how a man contracted to do a bit of homesteading. Or rustling—Kelly grinned at that thought. A claim was no good without something to use its water and grass.

Having not the remotest idea as to where Running Iron lay in relation to this place, he headed back to Abbie's. When he got there, Colorado was in the soddy, as occupied as Abbie with the new member of the household.

"By gum, Kelly, said Colorado, "you forgot to bring along this boy's tongue."

"Why, he can talk," Kelly retorted. "Can't you, pardner?"

"Son of a bitch," said Jimmy, thus encouraged.

"Why, Jimmy!" Abbie gasped.

The boy, growing excited, pointed his fingers at Colorado. "Bang—gut shot!"

"I reckon," Colorado reflected, "that I catch on to why his ma wanted to farm him out."

Kelly grinned. "Abbie'll either cure him of that, or he'll have her acting the same way. How does a rider get to Running Iron?"

From the way the other eyed him, Kelly understood that Colorado knew all about Badger's homesteading idea and the man he hoped to persuade to attempt it.

"Dead easy," said Colorado. "Just point your nose east and follow it."

"Might not be back for a while," Kelly told Abbie.

Maybe she didn't like that, or maybe she didn't care a whit. He couldn't tell.

By the time he came in to Badger Gamble's headquarters, Kelly had gained a good impression of this mother-hen ranch from which the collection of activities against the big outfits had been conducted. It lay along another of the little creeks that fingered through the hills.

Except for being a little larger, it could have been Abbie's place, with no advantages not shared by its neighbors. Kelly wondered why there was any need for Colorado's services as a ramrod, then derived a fair answer for himself. Much of Badger's work had to do with the colony as a whole. The homely Colorado was probably his second in command in that wise, also.

Badger had seen him coming and was waiting in front of the soddy, apparently the only man on the place.

"Where's this here land office?" Kelly said bluntly.

Badger grinned. "By God, I knowed you'd come through. Step in and help me drink a batch of coffee before it eats through the pot."

The sodhouse showed strict bachelor tenancy yet was entirely neat. Kelly didn't know what time it was, but Badger had just eaten a meal. They sat down at the table with the coffee.

"Lot to be done," Badger reflected, "and we got to move fast. First thing is to get you an iron-clad claim to that vacant piece. Then get the boys humping to build a fence along the correct line between it and Horse Track. Finally we got to bring you in a bunch of steers."

"Now, wait a minute. I ain't even got the money to winter myself, let alone buy steers."

Badger Gamble waved a dismissing hand. "My barn's already full of bob-wire and fence posts we sneaked in some time ago. As for steers, what's wrong with a Chance Comber start, the same as the rest of the boys

67

made? We got mebbe two or three weeks before Chance'll get round to setting up his winter organization. The hitch has been in finding us a man for that spot. There I been a mite uneasy."

"If you think I know what you're driving at, you're crazy."

Badger grinned at him. "We got to fence your north line, and the east and west lines back to the bluff. You been up there, I reckon. Did you get down to the camp?"

"There was a pretty good trail down from the rim."

"And it's the only one on that whole bluff a steer would risk its neck on. So you can locate your stuff up on the bench. It'll soon learn to go down to water, then turn around and come back up on top. Fence and bluff combined would make you a dandy in-pasture."

"Wouldn't the buildings still be Horse Track's?" Kelly asked.

"The way I understand it, a man puts a building on land he don't own and he's got to leave it there. Anyhow, what could he do unless he knows how to move a hole in the ground?"

"What he can do," Kelly said, "is blast me the hell off of there and rip out the fence."

"Which I don't think he'll try till he knows where he stands. There's where mebbe I got another ace up my sleeve. His plans for cleaning out the nester colony have been based on the use of hired killers and dummy squatters he can disclaim any connection with. As long as there's no clear-cut violation of the federal land laws, he's got nobody to worry about but the county authorities, which same he now controls."

Kelly nodded, his eyes beginning to gleam. "But he can't wait for that rigamarole when he's out a big piece of winter grass he's got to have quick."

"And can't get back," said Badger, "without coming out into the open. Which is when we invoke federal law and get a deputy marshal in here."

"And you hope he does just that," Kelly accused.

"Mebbe," Badger admitted. "Ain't it time we reminded a few people this is still part of a civilized nation? Terry Kilrain has vanished. Charlie Redd is dead, and we think we know who back-shot him. There's plans for multiplying them murders ten times. And it's become my policy to beat Chance Comber and his high-and-mighty cronies at their own game."

"How about going to the state and asking it to step in."

"You can't do that," said Badger, "unless you can convince it a state of anarchy exists. Which is something we can't do as yet. Not unless we can bait 'em into a lot more carelessness than they've showed so far."

"Badger," Kelly said, "I don't see no horns, but are you sure you don't have a tail?"

"Just a hind end that drags some at my age."

"You sure don't let any grass grow under it."

"Comber won't, either, if he finds out he's lost his south line camp. That water controls a mighty big piece of his home range. He'd either have to abandon all the rest of that grass, sink some wells in nothing flat, or let his stuff wear off its fat trotting back and forth to the Cactus Branch, which is the closest stream."

"A mean trick," Kelly reflected, "if played on anybody but him."

"You get this straight," Badger said firmly. "All we ever done to Comber was make him pay his honest bills. Nobody in this colony has ever made a dishonest dollar. Or intends to. When the account is squared, we call it off."

"You going to the land office with me?"

"I better. It's quite a trip, and we better get riding. We'll go past Virg Partch's and tell him to have the boys lined up to start building fence like beavers just as soon as it can be done legal."

CHAPTER 8

THE CHUNKING OF THE MAULS IN THE HANDS OF ARMED and eager men was loud to Kelly's ears. Helping Virg Partch string barbed wire on the fence posts already set, he admitted privately to considerable nervousness. They had a man down on the western approach to the big flat to look out for Horse Track riders. But Kelly had the sneaking feeling he would as leave have them discover this new fence while he had the nesters here to side him.

Just the same, now the claim was his. He kept reminding himself of that and trying to feel some pride of ownership. It wouldn't come because his visit with Badger to the land office had only been a legal step. The real ownership hinged on who could hold the claim, which had yet to be determined.

Virg Partch was a runty man with a wide, good-natured mouth and the devil's own recklessness in his faded blue eyes. He had ridden for Horse Track until he got sick of helping Chance Comber get richer, he said, and had once wintered in this very line camp.

"If I hadn't gone and married a school marm," he commented, "I'd have wanted this claim myself. But I reckon you'll allow it would be no life for a woman."

By sundown of that first day the fence was built. The sweaty but elated crew gathered in the half-soddy for coffee, courtesy of Horse Track. Afterward Badger

70

suggested that Kelly spend the night on Running Iron with him. There remained a chore or two to be done before he set up housekeeping on his spearhead homestead.

Day had vanished when they rode in to Badger's headquarters. Both men were dead tired and were silent as they attended to the horses. They had a quick supper, then went to bed.

Early the next morning they were back in the saddle, leading a pack horse and riding northeast. All Kelly knew was that they were going after his cattle, about which Badger had little to say. They rode straight across country, toward the ford of the Standing Rock.

When they had crossed the valley's main stream, Badger bent their course more westerly, leaving Kelly to understand that so far they had mainly been bending around Horse Track's frequented range. They pressed forward steadily through the long, hot afternoon. The country began to change, and Kelly realized they were getting into a kind of badlands region.

They camped that night at a waterhole Badger brought them to with practiced ease. Early the next day they reached a watered coulee deep in the uninhabited roughs. The floor of the space was covered with yearling steers, around a hundred head. They wore crude, running bands that looked like an arrow until the light dawned in Kelly's mind.

"The Spearhead!" he exclaimed.

Badger chuckled. "So far an unregistered brand. You want it?"

Kelly sat his saddle in sheer amazement. He knew it was an old rustler trick to gather a hideout bunch under some unregistered brand. In the event of discovery, the rustlers could disclaim any knowledge, let alone possession, of the

71

brand. But if the steal seemed to work, the cattle could be moved and the brand made official.

"Horse Track slicks?" he asked.

"That's what they are. Colorado and the boys spent most of last winter gatherin' 'em."

"And I'm supposed to register the brand in my name?"

"It's safe enough. Chance knows he's losing calves right along. But so far there's been no sign he ever stumbled onto this cut. It's too far away. Anyhow, he'd never be able to prove that you not only took his line camp but stocked it with his stuff overnight. Not even with the help of a hireling sheriff."

"I'd sure have to show somebody a title."

"I already got you one. A cattle dealer who has reason to hate Comber has obliged more than once before. That's how we've managed to keep Chance plumb frustrated."

Kelly's back had stiffened. "Look here, Badger. You're leading me into a life of crime, safe or not. Comber's given me trouble, but he don't owe me a cent. You boys are collecting from him. Me, I'd be stealing any way you looked at it."

"If you hadn't said that," Badger returned promptly, "I'd of been a mite uneasy about you. So you would be. But mebbe you wouldn't mind doing a little collecting for Abbie, and Comber still owes her plenty."

"What if I want my own steers?"

"Then marry the girl," Badger said cheerfully, "along with her steers and accounts receivable."

"You old matchmaker. If you think so much of the institution of marriage, how come you never teamed up with some gal?"

"I've lived to learn I should of."

By nightfall they were on the long drive back. The Spearheads were wild, having been left unattended, Badger said, after they had been settled on this lonely, hidden range. The drive stopped overnight on the site of the previous camp, the next morning hurrying on south. Kelly's tensions began to make themselves felt again as they drew nearer to the Standing Rock ranges.

The distance riders could cover in a day greatly exceeded the mileage a traveling herd could make, no matter how hard it was shoved. Yet the enforced slowness did not seem to trouble Badger nearly to the extent that it wore on Kelly. Thus Kelly was the more alert when trouble came out of the seeming quietness.

They were by then well into the valley, skirting a string of haystack buttes that gave some concealment from the lower reaches of the valley. They were abreast one of these bare, sandy land crowns when the punching report of a carbine shot rang out.

Kelly could see nothing, and they were fully exposed to the gunman, with no place to take cover. This fact was flashing into his mind when he heard a coughing grunt behind him. Fear twisted his nerves as he jerked about in the leather just as Badger let go and flopped out of the saddle. The spooked horse wheeled away from the old man, clearing the boot from the stirrup. In the same interval there came a second carbine shot.

Heedless of his own safety, Kelly saw the ambusher, up where the butte line broke clean against the brassy sky. Fury drove in his spurs for him and, as his horse sped forward, he plucked his gun. The waylayer must have left his own mount on the back side of the elevation. Flattened now on the back of his horse, Kelly swung to the right, hoping to whip around in time to prevent the man's retreat.

As he came around the butte he was momentarily cut off from the man's sight. He spotted the horse, a Horse Tracker, just as the now concerned gunman fired again. The bullet squawled in Kelly's ear. Kelly's eyes narrowed bitterly. The man, now bent on keeping possession of his horse, was Smiley Dennis. Kelly fired just as Dennis lifted the carbine to shoot once more. The man threw up a hand, falling, the weapon flying through the air to kick up dust when it hit the ground. The man was down and still.

Kelly had a queasy, dreadful wonder as to how long Dennis had been watching him and Badger, how much he had guessed about the origin of the Spearheads now bolting on. He didn't know but what there was somebody else, waiting and watching this also.

Yet there was a good chance, he realized as the shock cleared a little from his mind, that Dennis might have stumbled onto this opportunity to get the nester leader. He was the vainglorious type of gunslinger who would find it hard to pass up.

He rode onto the butte to look at the gunhand and make sure be wasn't playing 'possum. But the man was shot through the head, already dead. Then, riding down to the level, Kelly sent his horse streaking back around the butte. He was thinking now of Badger and dreading what he might find. He saw as he came around that the steers were still pelting forward but holding together. That didn't matter much now.

He dismounted beside the still figure on the sandy earth and dropped to his knees. Badger's shirt, at the shoulder, was drenched with bright red blood. Kelly felt considerable relief at the discovery, realizing the impact, combined with the skittering horse, had dislodged Badger from the saddle. The fall had knocked him out cold.

Kelly stood staring down at the man, feeling an enormous respect for him and something warmer and more intimate. Badger had offered him a real friendship, based strictly on his judgment of character. He'd entrusted vital information and responsibilities to a virtual stranger on the strength of that judgment. Kelly felt more than gratitude, he harbored a deeper sense of responsibility than had been in him before.

He tore strips from his shirt to bind up the wound, trying to stop the bleeding. Blood began to come back to deepen the brown of Badger's whiskery cheeks. Presently his eyes slitted open and he let out just one short, repressed groan.

"You all right, Kelly?"

"Still holding together. That was one of Comber's new gun crew. And was is correct. I got him."

"How about the steers?" Badger returned, as if attaching no importance to himself.

"They're still pedaling for yonder."

"Well, catch my cayuse, and let's get riding."

Kelly agreed as to the stark necessity of that. "Sure you can stick it?"

"I ain't unstuck yet."

Kelly caught Badger's horse, which had quit running and started to graze about a mile south of the shooting. When he got back with the animal, Badger was sitting up, smoking a cigarette. He'd been hit in the left shoulder and so was able to swing aboard without help. Then they rode out at a quickened walk, the fastest gait Badger could stand, to overtake the steers. Once they had caught up with the animals, it did not take Kelly long to bunch them better and get them moving again under control.

Yet by the time they reached the Standing Rock

75

crossing, Badger's face was twisted with pain and he rode in a slump. No man alive was tough enough to take a major gunshot wound and throw it off with a grin and a shrug. Kelly wanted to abandon the cattle and get him on home, but Badger wouldn't hear to it. Kelly threw the bunch across the river, and they went doggedly, slowly on.

Virg Partch, who had been asked to look after things, was waiting when at last the little drive reached the Running Iron. By then Badger was only half conscious, and Virg helped Kelly carry him into the soddy. But the wound was not bleeding much by then. It was shock that had the nester leader in its grip. They laid him on his bunk and covered him with blankets, while Kelly explained what had happened.

"I don't think Dennis had been doggin' you," Virg said, although he looked plenty worried. "So there's a good chance he's the only one who got a look at them Spearhead steers coming down from up north. It was just a gunman's chance, and the jeebo jumped at it. But he's upset things plenty. We've got to reorganize."

"First we got to get a doctor."

"I'm thinking of that. You cut over to Abbie's and send Colorado on to town. Afterwards, he'll have to stay here and run things till Badger's back in harness. So you'll have to take Colorado's place riding herd on Abbie, it looks like."

"I'll fetch the doctor," Kelly put in, "and pinch-hit for Badger, myself."

"You scared of that little half-pint of woman?"

"I got a homestead of my own," Kelly snapped.

"Which is closer from her place than from here. Son, you're euchred. Get on with it, now. As soon as I can, I'll run the Spearheads on over there."

"Badger said he had a bill of sale for 'em. Which same I want in my possession before I put them Spearheads on land officially registered in my name."

"I'll fetch it."

The hour was growing late when Kelly reached the little Kilrain headquarters. There was a break in that, for Colorado was in and washing up for supper. He saw Kelly's lack of a shirt and let his jaw drop in surprise.

"You had a ruckus?" he breathed.

Kelly told him what had happened. By the time he was through, Abbie was standing in the doorway, listening in tight-faced interest, Jimmy staring bashfully around her slim legs. Hanging up the towel, Colorado wheeled toward the corral to get his horse, but Abbie called him back and made him eat. Yet that requirement delayed the homely puncher but little, and he was soon thundering out on the long ride to Lone Point.

While Kelly finished his own supper, he was aware of the deep concern in the girl. Maybe she knew Badger had been thinking of her and her aloneness in the world. Perhaps she even realized that the Spearheads were another collection he was making on the debt Comber owed her father. Or it could be she didn't like the thought of being too much alone with Kelly Drake after Colorado had returned to the Running Iron.

"How you making out, Jimmy?" Kelly asked the boy playing on the floor.

Jimmy looked up and grinned. "Son of a gun," he answered.

"You been making headway," Kelly told Abbie.

"The things Rio Bell must have taught him," Abbie breathed. "Why would any man do that to a child?"

"Mainly, I reckon, Rio was doing it to Linda," Kelly

reflected. "I'm worried about her, Abbie. She's going to come to a hard end if she sticks to that bugger."

"Then why does she stick to him?"

"She figures she's used up her rights to swap men."

"I don't see it that way at all," Abbie said defensively. "Any woman can lose her head about a man she knows isn't good for her. If she comes to her senses again, she's got a right to try and undo the damage."

"You ever lost your head over a man who wasn't good for you?"

Her cheeks flushed. "I don't intend to lose my head over any man alive. But that doesn't keep it from happening." Afterward she was preoccupied, lost within herself.

Finally, when he was convinced that it did not all have to do with him, he said, "Abbie, something's eating on you. What is it?"

"Well, Ty Hemrick came by today on his way home from town. He had news. Rio Bell has appointed himself a new deputy." Bitterness flooded her face. "Trench Durnbo—one of the men who killed my father. Isn't that irony for you?"

It was a lot worse than that, Kelly thought in spurting anger. It was callousness beyond belief. Yet it made sense from Rio's viewpoint. Combined, the two of them would make a wicked team for anybody to have to deal with.

"I know how you feel," he groaned and wished there was something he could do about it.

He found one of Colorado's shirts and he slept in the barn, that night, or tried to sleep. The day's tensions were hard to throw off, and bewilderment began to compound in him about the future and the chances the nesters had of surviving in a country so completely without honest law.

It had begun to look like he would have to do everything possible to goad Chance Comber into laying himself open to federal law. Where before Kelly had felt dread of that conflict, he began to feel eager for it. He knew this was a dangerous frame of mind that easily could sweep him into utter recklessness. But Badger's shrewdness became increasingly evident. The local law was being swiftly armed for violence of the bloodiest sort.

Abbie was cooking breakfast when he walked over to the soddy the next morning. Jimmy was still asleep in the bedroom. Kelly washed up at the outside bench. When he went on in, Abbie was taking up the meal. She was constrained, and he knew this arrangement wasn't going to work. She didn't like the idea of living alone with him. Maybe it came only from a sense of propriety, or maybe it stemmed from more. She seemed relieved when he announced his intentions of looking over the range. Under the circumstances, he was almost as relieved to get away.

In Ogallala she had made it perfectly clear that she had no use for a Texas man. But since then he'd proved himself to be of a cut different to the ones Comber had been hiring to fight her and her friends. He had gotten into a few scrapes another man might have stepped clear of, and he'd kept on building himself a reputation as a gunmaster in doing it. But he loathed a gun when it had to be turned on a man of any stripe, and she had ought to give him that much credit. She thought he was itchy-footed without conceding that, given enough reason, he might be otherwise. It seemed to him that, mainly, she just liked to be contrary.

He did the small amount of outriding required on a spread the size of hers, but he took plenty of time with it. He managed to keep busy until noon, when he went in for a meal.

They were eating when, for long seconds, the interior of the soddy was illuminated by the flickering run of a heat lightning flash that made Abbie and Jimmy jump. Even harder on the nerves was the rolling peel of thunder that crashed across the hills. At once an unnatural dusk swept in, to be split time and again by the bright sky anger. Then came the rain.

It fell in a torrential curtain, drumming sound on the hut's flat roof and bouncing as it bit the parched ground. Jimmy began to match the thunder peals, using his fingers for pistols, making targets of Abbie and Kelly.

"One gunman's enough around here," Abbie snapped and caught him up. "Time for your nap."

Jimmy protested loudly, but they disappeared through the curtain into the bedroom. Abbie was gone a long while, either trying to get the boy asleep or succumbing to it, herself. Chill had come with the downpour, and Kelly freshened the fire. He poured more coffee and stared into the flames while he smoked a cigarette, reflecting on her tart comment.

She was just coming out of the bedroom when the lightning struck. Kelly was aware only of a blinding flash that shook the structure and the feeling that he had been hit in the back of the head with a red-hot sledge. But his senses cleared when he saw Abbie stagger forward and fall. He reached her in a single bound, smelling the reek of sulphur in the room, knowing that they had taken one dead close.

He got his hands under her limp body and picked her up. Her mouth came open as her head fell back, but he

80

could see the breathing in her breast. He experienced a giddy relief in seeing that she had only been knocked down and stunned. He carried her to the cot that stood against the wall and put her down.

She was warm and soft in his arms, and he didn't immediately withdraw them. There wasn't any disrespect in him, just a wonderful tenderness. But when she opened her eyes she scrambled away from him as if she had been caught in the coils of a snake.

Anger went all through him. "I wasn't fixing to ruin you!" he bawled.

She sat up, and maybe it was only the electric shock that flushed her cheeks that way.

"I'm sorry," he muttered. "You feel all right?"

"I guess. Jimmy—?"

"I'll see about him."

Jimmy hadn't even awakened.

Only then did they realize that somebody had ridden up outside. Striding to the room's one window, Kelly looked out to see that there were two slickered riders with rainwater streaming from their hats. He recognized one at once as Colorado. Then he was boiling out the door, oblivious to the rain.

"Jim! You skunk-eatin' old Siwash. You green-gilled old gallywumpus!"

It was Jim Oliphant who swung out of the saddle with Colorado. The two men came on into the soddy, pegging their wet garments on the wall by the door. Jim's face was dead sober as he turned around and looked at Kelly. Colorado must have told him that his son was here. That was the uppermost thing in the puncher's mind right now.

Without waiting to be introduced, Abbie said, "In the bedroom, Jim."

They let Jim Oliphant go in alone to see his son. Apparently Jim didn't disturb the sleeping boy for there was no sound. Yet it was a long while before he came back out, an eased and more cheerful looking man. Abbie had made fresh coffee by then. The men sat down with it.

"Well, I had a time finding you," Jim said to Kelly. "Traced you finally to Kearney only to get the job of tracing you back to Ogallala and then on to Lone Point."

So that was the reason for the man's long delay in arriving. The loyalty it evidenced meant a lot to Kelly. They brought each other up to date, then. When he finally reached Lone Point, Jim had been given Kelly's letter, had been sufficiently impressed by it to head out to Running Iron immediately. Then Kelly told his own side of it, but nobody mentioned Linda's name.

"And I know what you're going to do for a while, Jim," Kelly announced. "Stay here with Abbie till Badger's on his feet."

Abbie looked surprised at the suggestion, and Kelly had a sudden wonder if she had been dead earnest when she piled out of his arms that way. But she was caught where she couldn't say anything about it, and Jim was little Jimmy's father. Anybody could tell from his face that he was as decent and trustworthy as Colorado, and not a man who would hold her too long just because she got knocked down by lightning.

"I'm obliged to you for taking care of him, ma'am," Jim told her. "And if I can be of any use to you, I sure hanker to do it."

"That would be the best arrangement," Abbie agreed, and her eyes avoided Kelly's.

"What you going to do then, Kelly?" Colorado asked.

"See what's left of my new ranch."

"Was I you," said Colorado, "I'd wait till this dew's burned off."

But the storm showed no sign of abating. Kelly wanted to have a little talk with Jim, and this was no place to do it. He said he guessed he'd go and get settled on Spearhead before dark. As he hoped, Jim followed him out to the stable.

Kelly told him then the things about Linda he had been unable to mention before the others, how she had given Jimmy up voluntarily, not expecting to see him again, of her obviously unhappy circumstances. But there was only a hardness in Jim's eyes as he listened. He had no comment to make.

"Don't be fool enough to figure Rio's your private meat, Jim," Kelly said finally. "The man's got a big thing going here, with a lot of good people threatened. You string along with us and don't get yourself murdered, too."

Jim only shrugged.

Saddling his horse, then, Kelly left at once, his coat collar turned up against the downpour, his face growing wet and chilled. He reached Spearhead in this torrent and found it as intact as when he had seen it last.

CHAPTER 9

THE RAIN STOPPED IN THE NIGHT. KELLY AWAKENED TO look out upon a land washed clean and misty now in the rising heat. He prepared his breakfast in satisfaction, his mind already busy with the things he had to do here before he was settled and ready to call himself a going concern.

It was around ten o'clock, with Kelly on the roof of the half-dugout repairing a leak the rain had disclosed, when he chanced to look to the west. He straightened in instant attention. A considerable cut of cattle was coming his way, from the wrong direction to be his Spearheads under the hazing of Virg Partch.

They had to be Horse Trackers, and he knew at once that Comber was starting to send out his winter herds to the line camps. The first real showdown over this piece of real estate had come.

He dropped off the roof, his breath running quick and shallow. He could hear the low, unhurried racket of the drive coming on, although now he could not see it. His muscles had tightened considerably when, seated on the chopping block in front of the house, he saw two horses running forward from the bunch at a gallop. He grinned thinly. They had caught sight of the barbed wire fence that had sprung up about the line camp they had meant to stock with cattle.

There was no polite greeting on the faces of the two who pulled up across the fence. Chance Comber's mouth was open, his eyes on fire. The other man was a stranger to Kelly, hard-eyed and full of fight, and probably a regular Horse Track puncher.

"What the hell's going on here?" Comber roared at Kelly.

Kelly rose lazily, mainly to let them make no mistake about there being a gun on his hip, the weapon Comber had already learned to respect.

He said, "Just a little homesteading, Comber. Nothing special."

"Who built this fence?"

"Me and some friends."

"It's old Badger's work," Comber fumed. "It's the first time that old bastard's tried any outright claim jumpin', and he sure as hell ain't going to get away with it!"

84

Kelly had a little trouble with the tightness in his throat. Comber looked ready to order that fence jerked out right now, and he had men along to do it. But Kelly didn't want that kind of thing from the man until Comber had visited the land office and been fully apprized of the way things stood. Presently, he could claim complete innocence of the fact that he was exceeding his rights.

"Just a minute," Kelly objected. "It happens I've made a legal filing on this claim, Comber. Go check at the land office and see. Then ask the commissioner what you can do about it."

"My line runs to that bluff!"

"That's what you thought," Kelly agreed. "But I'm telling you it runs where that fence does. You get the legal description, then measure it off from the other claims and see for yourself. That's what we done."

Comber straightened in the saddle. "You're lyin'."

"Better make sure before you get rambunctious, man."

His easy insolence seemed to convince Comber that he knew what he was talking about. Frustration tangled with the temper in the cattleman's face. He made a sweeping motion with his arm.

"This whole range depends on that waterhole! Without that, it's a complete loss!"

"I reckon you got a right to file a contest," Kelly agreed. "But of course that takes time."

"It's Badger's doin'!" Comber fumed, which fact alone seemed to persuade him that the matter should be looked into before he acted too heedlessly.

"You might say he sort of acted as my locator. But I done the filing, and I'm here to stay."

"We'll see about that." The man whipped his horse

about and was gone, his rider following. When they rejoined the bunch, Comber turned it back. He had no alternative until somehow he had provided water. The rest depended on his frame of mind after he had investigated the facts.

And if I'm going to be beefed, Kelly reflected, I better make certain I'm in the right.

He was thinking that he had better return voluntarily anything Horse Track could claim justly. He fell to work, first carrying the furnishings from the soddy and dropping it on Comber's side of the new fence. He followed that with the cooking utensils and small stock of provisions he had found on hand. He felt easier with all that moved across the line.

He was developing a possessive attitude toward his new property at last. It could never amount to more than a frying pan and coffee pot outfit, but that was about all any puncher could hope to achieve for himself. Unless he did plenty of mavericking. Kelly grinned, beginning to get a whiff of the heady scents Badger and the other nesters followed. There was still lots of public range about, once it could be wrested out of the control of big outfits like Horse Track, Zigzag and M Bar. He had as much right to it as they did.

But right now he had to get his own camp outfit and a supply of grub. That meant a trip to town. He'd have to borrow Badger's pack horse, and anyhow he wanted to see how the man was coming along.

He was getting ready to saddle up when he heard somebody's hail. Glancing up at the rim behind the place, he saw Virg Partch sitting his horse up there.

"Hey, you orey-eyed Texan!" Virg shouted. "I brung your steers and also a fancy title."

Kelly was glad to see the man but wished he hadn't

86

showed up just yet. He saw Virg eye in surprise the heap of things he had put across the fence. Then the man rode on to the place where the rim broke and let down in an easy descent. A few minutes later he rode up.

"What in hell's busted loose?" he asked.

"Chance Comber started to set up his winter camp," he reported. "And changed his mind when I pointed out some pregnant facts. Incidentally, how does a fact get pregnant, Virg? I was always puzzled about that."

"They get that way," said Virg, "from ring-tailed galoots like you and old Badger."

Kelly explained why he'd decided to clean all of Comber's legitimate property out of the dugout, and his own need to go to town on a buying trip. The arrival of the Spearheads was a little untimely, but Virg said he would stay overnight and keep an eye on things. He'd told his wife he might not be back that night.

"And I reckon old Chance can spare me a couple more meals," he reflected, eyeing the provisions beyond the wire. "Anybody who rides for that old skinflint does sixty dollars worth of work for his thirty-and-found. Then don't get much found."

"How bad's the loss of this range going to hurt that man?" Kelly asked. "Badger don't tell anybody more than suits him at the time."

"As one of his ex-riders," Virg said, "it'll hurt Horse Track plenty. And Comber knows better than you and me that Badger's sure to come up with something else. One of these times it's going to occur to him he'd better square up with the people he's cheated and robbed if he wants to stay in the cattle business. Or else he's going to go on the prod and lay himself open to justice for the first time in a snake-track career. Either one would suit Badger fine."

"It'd be easier on me, I allow, if he just squared up."

"Which he won't, and here's your title to the steers."

The paper Kelly took from Virg was made out to him. "How's this going to help Abbie collect from Comber?" he asked.

"I reckon Badger figures on letting nature take her course."

"I never seen a country," Kelly breathed, "so anxious to get a man in trouble."

Having little time to waste now, he saddled up and rode up to the top of the rim. He grinned when he saw the little tag of Spearheads, already spreading out on their new grass. He had never made the ride from there to Running Iron, but Partch had given him directions. Lifting his horse to a mile-eating clip, he headed in that direction.

Affairs on Running Iron were normal and placid, he found. Colorado was out somewhere doing the ranch work. Badger was up and about, belittling his injury but obviously handicapped by it for a considerable time to come. Kelly stayed only long enough to throw the wooden saddle onto a pack horse, meanwhile reporting Comber's visit to Spearhead.

Badger was pleased with the way the new owner had set the man back. But he counseled redoubled caution. Comber had a lot of tricks in his bag, Badger said, as he himself had learned expensively.

Kelly reached Lone Point in late afternoon, put up his horses and again registered at the hotel. He went straight to the mercantile afterward and did his buying, ordering the stuff sent to the livery so he could load up and be on his way home the first thing in the morning. Back on the street, he saw nothing to cause him concern. Yet he was uneasy and realized at last that this came from his concern for Linda. He knew that, deep in his mind, he still had a hope of seeing her again.

He went to a restaurant and had his supper. Returning to his hotel room, he remained there, rolling cigarettes and smoking them, while dusk and then full night came in upon the town. A little after dark, he left the room and went out again.

The lamps threw their pale light across the night. The hitching bars had been cleared of wheeled vehicles now, but there were more saddlehorses. His gaze strayed in the direction of Rio Bell's house. He would go there again if he could get a line on Rio's whereabouts that encouraged him. He figured the Longhorn saloon would be a good place to try for that. He would go there and kill some time, maybe get into a modest game to cover his deeper interests.

He found the place half filled, quiet. A game happened to be forming at the end of the room, the men displayed by the falling lamplight wearing range clothes. Kelly approached with a genial manner.

"Any chance to set in?" he asked.

They all looked at him with some surprise yet even more curiosity. Probably he was getting to be something of a notorious character, because he placed none of them.

"Sure, why not?" one of them said.

Kelly took a seat.

He didn't know how much time had passed when he grew aware of a stir of interest about him. Men had come and gone in the casual game, and he had held his own without much caring. He looked up, but all he saw immediately was the puncher across from him, who had lifted his glance to somebody behind Kelly.

"Howdy, Sheriff," the man said and grinned.

Kelly fought the stiffening of his shoulders, not wanting to show his sudden worry. The cowpoke across the table had a hard slash of a mouth. Kelly wondered suddenly if he was another regular Horse Track rider. Then the man's eyebrow made a funny little movement. Kelly sprang to his feet, stepping wide.

Rio Bell had a look of amusement on his face and something more, a waxing ugliness. Charlie Redd's old sheriff's badge was pinned to his vest, and the sight of it was galling to Kelly.

"Matter, Drake?" Rio murmured. "Somebody goose you?"

The flush in Rio's cheeks showed he had been drinking. The badge had put a considerable confidence in him. He was a different man to the one who had come to Kelly's hotel room, that night, moved by fear of being exposed and ruined. The same thought, growing in Kelly's mind, gave him a picture of Redd, who might have been shot in the back by this man, a definite image of Linda with her face bruised and swollen.

"I don't like a killer at my back, Rio," Kelly said quietly.

He heard somebody's sucked-in breath.

Rio must have learned of his presence here and come to crowd trouble. Kelly was ready to meet it, and his gaze clashed into Rio's with steady hostility. The inevitable space began to clear quietly about them as men edged back.

"That's a strong remark," Bell all but whispered.

"But still not strong enough."

The spoiling eyes of Rio belied his chilly grin. He whirled in and he threw a punch.

Kelly hadn't looked for that, but he was no more afraid of it than of Rio's gun. Rio was the bigger man by physical standards, and he was hardened and tough. The blow caught Kelly in the belly, forcefully enough to knock out a gust of air.

The wall Kelly had turned his back to now held him up. His spread arms pressed the boards, and he straightened up. Rio might have hurt him badly in that moment but he waited warily. The man had stopped grinning, his mouth slipped back into its natural surliness. His lips tightened, then he punched overhand with a swift and vicious swing of his shoulders.

But Kelly was under it, his own left streaking out. His feet danced lightly, and he had recovered from that initial daze. He laced into Rio, driving blow after blow, and the man went down. The onlookers saw that it was to be a hard fight and enlarged the circle.

Nobody seemed to hear the bartender's shouted objections. Rio hit the sawdust on his gluteals, then his elbows, the fall broken by the sawdust cushion. His face twisted bitterly as he shoved up. He stood for a moment in sudden caution. His head bobbed to one side, then straightened as he scowled.

"Hello, handsome," Kelly jeered. "Too bad this deadfall's got no women to see you get up off your fancy pants."

Wariness remained in the hatred Rio let show plainly. He stepped sidewise, head cocked, studying his enemy. Then he bored forward, and Kelly was slammed hard against the bar. The impact shook the room, rattling the back bar. Rio began to pull and chunk his fists forward and back in a steady assault, rising on his toes as he sought to end it.

Kelly barely survived the attack. He could only slide along the bar in an effort to break out of the trap. Rio slugged more wildly, made a kick at Kelly's crotch. Then Kelly came into the clear.

His confidence increased, Rio bore on. But now Kelly was better set. He met the rush. The impact as they came together shook him, but he sledged a blow to the man's ear in a hooking drive. One of Rio's feet left the floor, the supporting knee bending. Kelly let go another blow, driving it crashing to Rio's mouth. He felt his knuckles tear, and he felt teeth break off. He brought away a bloody fist, but Rio was going down. The man hit the sawdust and did not try to get up. Then his eyes rolled up in their sockets, and he was limp.

Kelly looked around fiercely, but nobody else was buying chips.

"I busted his handsome mouth," he panted. "Somebody better lug him to the sawbones."

Finding his hat, he walked out.

CHAPTER 10

HE MADE HIS WAY TO THE HOTEL AT ONCE BUT DID NOT enter. When a quick back glance showed him that he had not been followed, he rounded the corner of the building. Reaching the back alley, he reversed his direction, moving with caution, remembering that this was the place where Linda had helped him out that night.

As he passed behind the Longhorn he could hear the excitement within. With a grim smile, he warned himself that he had crowded his luck in that establishment to the utmost. Nor did Kelly Drake mean to push it elsewhere again. He moved on cautiously, not returning to the main street until he was at the south end of the town. There he crossed the main thoroughfare hurriedly, seeing no signs of pursuit. He pressed on to the creek.

He came in behind the Bell house along the same route he had followed before. There was no light, there or in the houses on either hand. He moved on with increased care, coming onto the rear porch of the place. He had to knock twice before he heard sounds of movement inside.

Her low voice called, "Who is it?"

"Kelly, Linda."

The door was unlocked. It swung open, and he saw her there in the darkness, undressed for bed and wearing a robe over her nightgown. He stepped quickly inside. The door latch clicked, then she clutched him.

"I thought you were a thousand miles from here," she said, and then was crying against his chest.

He had only wanted to check on her, when he came here, but now a decision became firm and fixed in his mind. Somehow he was going to get her away from this, tonight.

"You all right?" he asked.

"Yes. Where's Jimmy?"

"Want to see him?"

"You—you mean I could?"

"Tonight, Linda. If you'll come with me. For keeps."

She stepped back. "I've no right."

"You're his mother."

"He—he misses me, too?"

"He sure does."

Kelly wasn't going to say anything about Jim's being up in the sand hills, knowing that would spoil his chances of persuading her to come there.

In a voice he could hardly hear, she said, "Rio would never let me get away."

"He don't love you that much."

"No," she admitted, with the bitterness of a woman

who has found that, at such cost to herself, she has only gratified a man's curiosity and passion. "But I know too much."

"Probably no more than I know," Kelly said harshly. "Linda, for Jimmy's sake if not your own, you've got to do it. There isn't much time. I don't reckon it'll hurt you to learn I spoiled that man's handsome mouth, tonight. Don't take time to do any more than get dressed. Then follow the crick south of town. I'll get horses and pick you up."

"Where'll we go? Where could I stay?"

"With friends of mine. They'll treat you right. Will you do it?"

Her tight, lingering silence told him better than words of the corner in which she was caught. The knuckles that had smashed Bell's mouth didn't hurt quite so much while he waited.

"He'll find and kill me," she said finally. "But I can't stand this. I've got to see my baby."

"You'll be up at the crick when I come along?"

The answer was a firm one, finally. "Yes, Kelly. I'll be there."

"Good. You got a gun?"

"Yes."

"Fetch it."

He left at once. Since time now pressed and this side street was wholly dark, he made his way directly to the main thoroughfare. When he reached the livery, which was just closing up, he found that his order had been delivered from the mercantile. The hostler responded to the five dollar bill Kelly thrust at him and helped to saddle the two animals, then to pack the lead horse. They were not quite finished when a man loomed in the livery's archway.

94

It was Trench Durnbo, still wearing his two guns and now with a deputy's badge boldly displayed on his grimy vest.

Kelly had whirled in a single reflex action and pulled his gun. It covered Durnbo before the man fully realized who it was he saw in the pale interior light.

"Come on in, Trench," Kelly murmured. "And don't let out a peep."

He had not yet asked for Linda's horse, not wanting to arouse curiosity in the liveryman. But concern came up in the fellow as he divined something of the true nature of the situation. He backed off.

"This looks like something I don't want any part of!" he bawled.

Kelly stepped back so that his gun could cover both of them. "All right. Then back into that tack room there. Both of you."

Durnbo's eyes glittered in their hostility, but he dared not refuse. The stableman retreated with alacrity, stepping into the harness room behind him. Durnbo followed. When he had entered after them, Kelly moved in warily and took Durnbo's guns. Stepping out with them, he shut the door and hasped it from the outside.

He had to take the first horse he came to in the stalls, then, and throw a saddle on it for Linda. His pulses crashed in his ears, but he worked in controlled speed. As yet there was no sound of general alarm on the street. But he knew that once more the town was turning into a deadly trap for him. He led the three horses out through the back door into the alley. He mounted.

For a moment afterward he listened closely. Already he could hear Durnbo's muffled bawling for help. Kelly had to let that go even though he realized the man would not stay locked up there very long. Leading the two animals he had with him, he started along the alley. At the first opening be turned to his right, moving directly out of town on the side opposite the creek.

He had to cut back to the road sooner than he felt safe, not knowing how far Linda would have got on foot, whether she was out here somewhere yet, or if she had lost her resolution and changed her mind. Crossing the wagon tracks, he rode on to the creek, thereafter following it at a slow walk.

"Kelly."

She stepped from the brush ahead of him. He saw in the pale starlight that she was dressed, wearing a skirt, sweater and a gunbelt with a weapon in the holster. But she had brought nothing else. He tossed her the reins of the other saddle horse. She was an expert rider, he remembered. She sprang up lightly, forking the leather in the way of a girl brought up on the range.

They walked their horses until they were out of earshot of Lone Point, then lifted them to a faster gait. Kelly meant to keep the pack horse, with the stuff he needed, as long as he could. But if there was pursuit, as he strongly feared there would be, he would have to let it go.

Linda was wholly silent, and he left her alone with her churning thoughts. It would only add to her disturbance to warn her that Rio's supporters had recovered their wits and taken up for the man.

When they had put some three miles between them and the town, he pulled down his horse. He was not surprised to hear, in the far rearward distance, the faint drum of massed hoofs.

"They're following us," Linda said quietly.

"Me," he corrected. "And mebbe it's a good thing I couldn't get your horse but had to steal one. There's nothing now to link your disappearance with me except the fact that I was in town at the same time. Did Rio tie me in with Jimmy's vanishing?"

"He thought I'd seen Jim secretly and let him have the baby. I let it go at that."

"Good. You and the boy'll be all right till he learns better. But that's only some of his cronies coming. We'll have to get off this road."

They bent to the right, where Kelly saw the pooled blackness of a draw between two hills. They had barely vanished into this concealment when a horseback party whipped past, sticking to the road. Although he did not know the country well enough to trust their safety to the monotonous, confusing hills, Kelly was afraid to return to the road after that. He took his bearings on the stars, did a little thinking, then they pressed on, passing through the draw into another hollow, then following that on a line he thought was parallel to the road. They traveled slowly afterward, it being more important to keep his bearings than to make time. Linda seemed to trust him completely, and he wondered if she had any lingering regrets for Rio Bell.

It was odd what made a woman give herself so completely to a man, yet he remembered Abbie's saying that any woman might do it.

He could not so much as surmise what it would be like if Linda and Jim saw each other again, as they would have to do if they both stayed in the nester colony. Jim's attitude toward his runaway wife had always been a puzzle to Kelly. No man could forgive the violation of his home, much less forget it. The question was where Jim's hatred lay and where lay his deep loyalties.

He decided to take Linda to Running Iron, which they reached in the breaking dawn. Kelly's shout, as they drew near, brought Colorado to the door of the soddy in his underwear. The ugly puncher pulled back hastily when he saw that one of the newcomers was a woman.

"There's a man," Kelly told Linda, "who's already broke Jimmy of cussing."

"Jimmy's here?"

"No. But you better stay here with old Badger Gamble. Likely you've heard of him, but if not he's as fine a man as ever lived. I'll fetch Jimmy over here as soon as I can. And there's something I better tell you. Jim's here, all right. Staying where the boy is."

"Jim's here?" Linda gasped. "Then I can't stay, Kelly—I just can't!"

"You don't need to see Jim. I'll tell him you're here, and leave the rest up to him."

"I can't face him."

"I don't have long white whiskers," he told her, "but there's one thing I've learned. A person can do a lot of things he don't think he can."

Colorado came out with his clothes on, Badger following. Kelly felt confusion climb in him, and he wished he had thought to ask Badger's permission for this, to explain it, beforehand.

Yet Badger seemed to recognize her, for he nodded his head and said, "Howdy, Missus Bell." He looked as puzzled as Colorado did.

"It's Mrs. Oliphant," Linda said. Suddenly she could hold up her head.

The light of understanding broke in the men's faces when she made that straightforward correction. They had heard the story in connection with Jimmy, and now old Badger's features creased in a smile.

"Linda," he corrected in turn, "and you're right welcome. We'll have us some breakfast."

"Thank you," Linda said. "Very much."

98

She seemed eased, as if she realized that she was with real friends for the first time in a long while, that also she was not condemned in their sight. She swung down and went into the house, realizing that Kelly wanted to talk with the men alone.

Kelly explained his action to Badger and Colorado, seeing at once that the step met with their approval.

"Not to turn hospitality into capital," Badger reflected, "but it won't hurt us any to have somebody on our side who knows a site more than we do about Bell's program."

"She could be a help," Kelly admitted. "But we won't crowd her. What help she gives ought to come voluntarily."

"Agree with you there," Badger said.

Kelly turned the pack horse over to Colorado to be picked up later, and headed out for Abbie's place. The morning sun moved up over the sand hills and became a notable heat on his back. He was dead tired, jaded, feeling excitement's inevitable aftermath. He saw smoke lifting from Abbie's chimney as he rode in. He reached the soddy to find her, Jim and young Jimmy seated at the table having breakfast.

He felt a deep uncertainty as he walked in.

"Anything wrong, Kelly?" Jim asked, staring at his face.

"Well, mebbe you'll think so, Jim," Kelly answered, searching his old saddlemate's eyes and finding no encouragement there. "I took it on myself to bring Linda out to Badger's. I promised her I'd bring Jimmy over. Don't get me wrong, Jim. It was all my own suggestion."

Darkness washed under the deep weathering of Jim's lean cheeks. "She's used up her right to Jimmy."

"She wanted to see him bad enough to humble herself and come out here."

Abbie took the question into her own hands. Looking at Jimmy quietly, she said, "Want to see your mommy?"

"Mommy," Jimmy repeated. Then suddenly his face changed as be seemed to grasp the idea. "Mommy—mommy!" Scrambling from his chair, he ran to the door.

"All right," Jim said, not looking at Kelly. "Take him over there. But bring him right back."

"Please, Jim," Abbie said, and she placed her hand on Jim's arm. "I know how you must feel, but find a little understanding in your heart."

"You ever had another man sleepin' with your wife?"

Her cheeks flushed. "I can understand why a woman would do it. And all I was going to suggest is that you let Jimmy stay with his mother. Badger's housebound for a while, and they'll be perfectly safe with him. Besides, Jim, Jimmy cries for her at night."

"Let him stay, then."

Jimmy was already outdoors hunting his mother and would not come back in. Abbie got together his things. Jim did not come with her when she brought them out. Kelly lashed the little roll to his saddle, swung up, then Abbie lifted up Jimmy.

The boy's face clouded as it dawned on him for the first time that he must leave this place to see Linda. He looked down at Abbie in uncertainty. His arms reached out to her, then he brought them back. He looked at the door of the sodhouse as if seeing beyond it the father he might not remember but now knew and liked.

The poor little cuss, Kelly thought. He just don't know who he likes the most. Why can't grown-ups use a little sense?

CHAPTER 11

COLORADO LOOKED WORRIED. "THAT CAYUSE YOU stole," he told Kelly, "could get you hung. And Rio Bell's just the sheriff that'd like to do it. What you going to do with the critter?"

Kelly shook his head dubiously. They were at Badger's barn, where he was picking up his pack horse for the trip on to Spearhead. The reunited child and mother were in the house, at this moment needing their privacy.

"You leave him here," Badger said. He was scratching his shaggy grey bead. "It's a Zigzag bronc, but God knows whose saddle you latched onto at the livery. Tonight Colorado can take the horse over and turn it loose on Zigzag range. We'll sneak the saddle back to town after the ruckus has simmered down a little."

Kelly was plenty willing to get rid of the dangerous horse Linda had ridden out from Lone Point. Leading the pack animal, he started out on the ride to Spearhead.

Virg Partch was waiting when he rode down off the rim and came into the old line camp. Nothing looked disturbed about the place, and Virg was easy in manner. But he wanted to get home, none of the nesters caring to leave their own places for long under the circumstances. He had soon disappeared over the rim.

Kelly unpacked the horse and took the stuff he had brought out from Lone Point into the dugout. He watered the animals, unsaddled and turned them loose in the fenced pasture below the bluff. The inevitable toll of his long ride and hard night made itself felt. The mere fact of being alone on this exposed edge of the nester colony disturbed

101

him. Comber was not the only man he was uneasy about. Rio Bell now was an even deadlier enemy. He stretched out on the straw-filled bunk. His torn knuckles hurt him, and he kept thinking of Bell and of Linda.

No matter what she had done, she was still slim and young and pretty, with a child to bring up and most of her own life still ahead of her. He couldn't see her as anything but clean and good, and he wondered how she had felt about his squaring things somewhat with Rio. Maybe she had not liked to hear that the man had had his handsome mouth broken. Women could be mighty queer and didn't always quit loving a man just because they had been hurt by him.

Maybe he had made a mistake. He could have killed Rio, or made a good try, for the man had expected a gunfight, had even wanted it. He had been spoiling for trouble, and Kelly Drake or somebody else had to kill him sooner or later. That was the only way a man like Bell could be stopped permanently.

He turned his rankling thoughts away from Rio and put them on Comber. The man had been hurt and thrown off stride by the unexpected loss of his main winter range, as Badger had wanted. But he might be too crafty to be caught in the trap Badger hoped to spring by taking action that would run him squarely afoul of federal law.

Comber had a tough crew of his own, bristling now with the trail hands he had hired in Ogallala. Of these, only Smiley Dennis had been eliminated. Comber had plenty of punch to throw when he had got back on balance.

Kelly awakened chilled by the growing evening, this change in the air reminding him again that fall was near. He was still drowsy and realized at once that it was the arrival of a horse that had aroused him. He shoved

102

hastily to his feet and buckled on his gun belt. He had climbed the dugout steps to the ground level when Colorado rode in.

"You have trouble with the Zigzag cayuse?" Kelly asked worriedly.

He had noted the deep concern on the puncher's face. But Colorado shook his head, not speaking until he had swung out of the saddle.

"Mebbe it's something worse. I dunno. Virg Partch come busting over to Running Iron, and Badger figured I ought to warn you. It looks like Corb Rivers has up and disappeared into thin air."

That was a nester Kelly had not yet met. He stared at Colorado, saying nothing.

With a sigh, Colorado resumed.

"Virg says he stopped by to see Corb on his way over here yesterday with the steers. Corb wasn't around. Stopped again on his way home, today, and Corb still ain't around. There was dirty dishes on the table the first time. They were still there, exactly the same way, the second time. Corb's in-stock was plenty thirsty. He ain't a man to pack off like that unless something made him do it."

"It sure don't look natural," Kelly admitted.

"Which makes it two to one something's happened to him."

"That what Badger thinks?"

"It's got Badger scareder than I ever seen him before." Colorado paused for a breath. "He figures mebbe this Spearhead stunt has backfired. Corb is one of the three homesteaders behind you. There's the Kilrain place, then Tansy Wooden's, to boot. So mebbe Comber's going to leave you plumb alone and slash deeper into the colony with this disappearin' business we can't figger out nohow."

"That wouldn't get him any water."

"It might put you in a frame of mind to trade water for a truce."

"It sure might," Kelly agreed with a groan. "You warned Jim Oliphant and Tansy Wooden?"

"Going there from here. But Corb could show up yet. I sure hope he does."

Colorado rode off immediately, leaving Kelly sick with apprehension. To keep anything from happening to Abbie, he would trade not only this waterhole but his life.

He cooked his supper, although he didn't have much appetite. His tensions would not ease. He was beginning to wonder if there wasn't a great deal more to the situation that either he or Badger had understood. If so, that extra could come from Rio Bell. Maybe Kelly Drake and Jim Oliphant were the only men in this country who knew of the snake tracks Rio had made down on the lower border. Certainly Charlie Redd hadn't known, and probably Chance Comber didn't understand that, either.

Yet he was wholly unprepared for it when Comber arrived at the line camp alone just at dusk. The man came without any show of hostility, and discretely remained on his own side of the new wire fence. He ignored his property, which Kelly had thrown over the day before.

Kelly was waiting in front of the dugout, not knowing what he had to face. He walked over to the fence, saying nothing at all, his eyes wary and belligerent as he stared at the cattleman.

Chance Comber looked like he had swallowed a rotten oyster. He gripped the reins with hands that showed white at the knuckles.

"All right, Drake. I'm ready to buy you off. What's your price for a quit-claim to this waterhole?"

"You checked?"

"I checked, and you hold the cards. I know better than poke a stick into a hornets' nest. How much do you want?"

"You're offering me money?" Kelly gasped. "That sure isn't what I expected, Comber. I figured to be dickerin' for Corb Rivers, if he ain't dead already. And Abbie Kilrain and Tansy Wooden."

Comber shot him a hard stare. "What about them?"

"Rivers seems to have vanished into the air, the way Terry Kilrain's body did." There seemed to be a complete lack of comprehension in Comber. Kelly was aware of that, bewildered by it.

"I don't know a damned thing about Corb Rivers."

Kelly believed him. The man was too disturbed to be feigning perplexity. Comber's face was dark with hurried thinking, like he had taken a blow and was trying to get his bearings again. Then suspicion came into his face.

"You trying to throw dust in my eyes?" he demanded. "I admit you got a legal claim to this waterhole. I got to have it. I'll be in a tight if I don't get it. But I got too much sense to blast you off of it the way things stand."

Kelly's laugh was not pleasant. "What made you think that money could buy me?"

"You don't look like a fool, Drake. You ain't fixing to settle on a two-bit cow spread for life. I know your breed. When you get itchy-footed again, you'll want another real riding job. You come from Texas, and so did I, way back. But I still got friends down there. I can get you blacklisted with every big outfit in that country or this."

Kelly had a sick feeling in his mouth. If Comber knew anything about Rivers, he surely wouldn't have come over here using any other kind of threat. Convinced, Kelly had but one other place to look for the new menace to the homesteaders whose claims backed his own. That was Bell, and whatever Rio was up to, he wasn't taking Comber into his confidence.

"I reckon my price is the same as Badger's," he said coolly. "You're squaring up for all the people you've cheated, skunked, killed or had killed."

Even that taunt failed to bring forth a threat to Abbie and Tansy Wooden. Comber's eyes were streaked with angry frustration. After a moment he shrugged and rode off. Kelly watched the rancher until he had vanished into the far dusk. It looked like Badger's seeds of fear were beginning to sprout in Comber. But new elements were entering the situation, dangerous and of unknown magnitude. One thing was certain. He was going to see Jim at once and stress the increased danger to Abbie. He didn't mean to lose any time about it.

Within ten minutes he was up out of the coulee and riding hard for the little Kilrain spread. The night was full now, the stars out and letting him see the underfooting well enough that he rode without trouble. His horse was still tired, but he forced it onward. Yet it seemed a long while before he could tell that he was getting close to Abbie's place.

He had dropped into a hollow and was following it when he heard the first sound of shooting in the distance. He was not himself exposed, but fear ran raw in him. His horse jumped forward as he dug in the steel, whipping up out of the hollow. He heard more firing, this time an angry outburst. He counted half a dozen shots.

106

Kelly was still slanting up the incline toward a point where he could round a butte and thus cross the last ridge. The firing had stopped, but in the next moment he caught the sound of horses whipping toward him. He swung abruptly to his right, coming in closer to the butte. As he pulled up there he could see, below in the starlight, the Kilrain sod structures.

Two horsemen came driving toward him, keeping lower down and aiming to bend around the butte. Kelly swung his horse until he was fully facing them. At that moment he realized he had been seen. The forward rider, still holding a pistol, chopped down with the weapon. A red, streaking flame showed in the night just as Kelly fired. The reports of two shots rolled together in the sand hills.

Kelly shot again. The forward rider jerked back in the saddle, teetered, then fell free and hard to the ground. His companion was bent low on the far side of his mount, disregarding his stricken saddlemate and seeming intent only on escape. Kelly sped two more shots after him, then the fleeing horse dropped into the hollow and out of sight.

Kelly forgot him instantly for the unloaded horse had swung hard to the right and cut back. Kelly was in instant pursuit. He had a hard run along the ridge before he caught the flying reins. It was a Horse Track animal, he saw when he could read the brand. Leading it, he went back to where its erstwhile rider lay. There was no sign at all of the first man. He had spooked, and Kelly was sure he was still burning distance to preserve his own hide.

The man on the ground was wholly motionless. As he hunkered down by him, Kelly could see him plain enough to recognize a man who had come up with one of the other herds from the south. One of Comber's Ogallala pickups, he realized, and the man was patently dead, shot through the neck.

Comber man on a Comber horse, Kelly reflected. Where did that put Comber now?

He did not have time to ponder the question. Moving hastily, he threw the dead man across the Horse Track horse. Then, leading that animal, he hurried down into the little basin, fearful now of what he might find when he got there.

When he was close enough to the soddy to be heard, he called, "Hello—it's me—Kelly!"

The door of the place did not open until he had ridden up. Then Abbie stood there, her father's rifle in her hand.

"Where's Jim?" he bawled.

"I don't know," she panted. "Colorado was here, then went on over to Tansy Wooden's. A little later we heard shooting in that direction, too close to be at Tansy's. I made Jim go. I thought somebody waylaid Colorado." Abbie caught a quick breath. "Then those two men came riding in. I drove them off."

"Thank God," he breathed. "How long before that did Jim go?"

"Long enough I was worried about him, too."

Kelly was also concerned for both men, but he knew he dared not leave Abbie alone again while he investigated. Somebody had been watching this place closely and had tricked Jim into leaving her unguarded. He wasn't going to give anybody a second chance at her.

"We'll have to keep wonderin' till daylight," he said. "But for what good it is, maybe we got something here. Attackin' this place was messing with federal law. I got a Horse Track cayuse and a dead rider that probably shows on Comber's payroll, to prove it happened. They

108

never figured on that. If you hadn't been on your toes, they'd have packed you off. The way I'm sure now they took Corb Rivers."

"I don't understand you," Abbie said.

"We got concrete evidence now that the land laws are being broken. Enough maybe we can get a marshal interested in what's going on in this country. Which will sure tie a knot in the tail of Comber if not in Rio Bell's."

Abbie shivered. "They'll try to get that evidence back, won't they?"

"They sure will. Or I'd be off trying to find out what happened to Jim and Colorado."

"We've got to get some kind of law," she said vehemently. "I'll never rest till I know what happened to my father's body. I guess I'd have found out too late, if you hadn't showed up. Thank you."

He put the Horse Track mount and its dead rider in the soddy stable. He hoped they would help to bring order back to his fermenting country. But stronger than that feeling was his relief that Abbie had managed to save herself. If they had hurt her—well, there wouldn't be a safe place on earth for anybody who ever did.

In the deep shadows of the earthen stable, he wondered for the first time what precise emotions made him feel that way about Abbie. He had grown convinced that the conflict between her and his wild, unruly nature was very real whether or not she sought secretly to stifle it. He would never change, nor would she, and it struck him suddenly how well she and Jim had hit it off.

Except for Linda, Jim would never have taken the trail north. His feet never seemed to itch, and it took a lot to put him on the prod.

Life could sure scramble people and throw them together in ironic, tragic ways.

CHAPTER 12

IT WAS IN THE FIRST BRIGHT STREAKS OF DAWN THAT Kelly saw Colorado riding leisurely to the Kilrain sodhouse. He was in the yard and bawling as the man came up.

"Ain't you seen anything of Jim?"

Colorado looked puzzled as he shook his head. "Not since I was here last night. Why?"

"They got him!" Kelly breather. "Sucked him away from here and latched onto him!"

"What you talkin' about?" Colorado demanded.

Kelly told him in swift, fierce words. "Look," he concluded. "You stay here with Abbie. I'm a fair hand at trailin', and I'm going to see what I can learn."

"You go ahead," Colorado said promptly. "I figured I'd spend the night with Tansy and did. We sure never heard any shootin, and we didn't have any trouble."

With no thought of his breakfast, Kelly headed for the stable. Everything was all right there. He saddled his own horse, his hands numb and clumsy in his haste, his mind too cold with renewed fear to think. He was soon riding out, west of Abbie's headquarters now. Jim didn't know this country well as yet. Instead of following the main trail to Tansy Wooden's, he'd probably struck out straight in the direction from which the shooting had come.

A little quartering west of the ranch structures let Kelly find the man's sign. He had guessed correctly, and Jim had headed straight up the long slant. As he followed, Kelly kept watching the forward distance. In view of the dangerous evidence left here, somebody might be watching the place already.

110

He topped the rise, the sign still easy to follow, for Jim had ridden hurriedly. Kelly rolled a cigarette as he rode, his face dark and scowling. He dropped down to the floor of the next hollow, and there found the place where Jim, beyond mistake, had run into trouble.

Three horsemen had waited on the blind side of the ridge, and Jim had bumped right into them. There was no sign of a struggle, so he must have ridden into three hostile guns. Kelly came to the tramped reminders of several horses. He saw where two of them had ridden on across the ridge and knew they had been the pair he tangled with after Abbie had driven them off. Two other sets of horse tracks moved north. That would be Jim and a man left to guard him.

At least Jim had not been hurt, not when he had been at this point. But that was of little reassurance to Kelly. Jim had bought chips in the game here by befriending and looking out for Abbie. Rio Bell had every reason to hate him. And maybe he had seen too much to be allowed to live when he had fallen into the deadfall.

Again Kelly rode sign with a dogged patience. He knew it would be wise to get help first, yet his fear for his friend's life made the time that would require a forbidding factor. At places on the sandy earth he could follow the horse tracks at a fast trot. Again he had to stop for a moment to puzzle.

Yet he made good progress. Jim's captor was heading north, and in that direction lay Comber's headquarters. That man had ought to be starred in a theatrical troupe, Kelly thought bitterly. He had surely acted innocent of any knowledge of this kind of dirty work. Kelly cursed him blue. The trail went on and on.

When he came to a halt, finally, he was atop a rise with the morning sun hard on his right. Far out on the flat below him he saw the willow and cottonwood of a big stream and, beyond them, the buildings and corrals of the first big ranch he had seen in this hill country. They were frame structures, attesting to the owner's prosperity.

From what hc had learned of the country, this was probably Horse Track. Yet it could be Murchison's M Bar. There were fenced pastures in which he could see both horses and cattle, too far off for the brands to be read. Whoever owned them, the tracks he had followed led on down toward the place, and he knew where Jim had been taken.

Kelly sat there through long moments in a seething impotence. It would be suicidal folly for him to go on in there alone. He could see nobody just then. But the horse corral showed a number of horses. He remembered that, after all, the day was just getting started. The best he could do was wait and see what he could learn. If enough of the crew rode out on regular ranch work, he might risk going on in. He swung his horse back to the blind side of the ridge, crossed again afoot and seated himself.

He was growing drowsy from this inactivity when he saw a party come out of the house together and head for the day corral. As they strung out a little, he counted four. He couldn't be sure at that distance but thought that one man had a gun on another. Kelly began to hear his pulse crash in his ears.

In a moment two of the men had entered the corral. Two stayed outside the fence, the one Kelly thought had a gun and the man he covered with it. Kelly was sure then, and his mouth was straight-ruled and bitter. His eyes narrowed in their hostile determination. He watched them saddle up. Then all were mounted and riding out. They headed east.

Kelly already had it figured out. They had brought Jim here for orders as to what to do with him. They had finished the night here, with no suspicion that they had been trailed, and now were going to carry out whatever orders they had received. Jim was still alive, which was something, but there was big trouble just ahead for him. Kelly aimed to be in on it when it came.

Slipping back over the ridge, he got his horse and went up to the leather. He could dog the party easily now and hunt for his chance. Eastward lay the first rises of the interminable sand hills, toward which his quarry was heading. The bare slopes reflected the sun. The party rode with a man in the lead, two abreast, then another behind. They moved at a steady gait, knowing where they were going, apparently, and meaning to get there without lost time.

Kelly followed on the blind side of the ridge mostly, climbing high enough for a look only now and then. Soon they passed out of view into the first hills. By then the ranch headquarters had fallen far behind. Crossing the ridge boldly, Kelly rode faster. But he watched the roundabout with close care.

The party he stalked was lost to view after that. Yet the sign, which presently he was following, was easy to see and stay with. It also was dangerous, he knew. If they got any warning of being followed, he could be blown out of the leather without knowing what had hit him.

The hills began to draw apart, a stream appearing that Kelly judged to be an affluent of the Standing Rock. The riders ahead had come down onto a well-worn horse trail that showed a less frequent passage of wagon wheels. That narrowed the possibilities as to where they were heading, and Kelly made his guess.

The forward country was opening into another long, narrow, trenchlike valley where there probably was another line camp belonging to Comber or another of the big operators. The impulse seized him to see if he could cut ahead of the party he followed, so as to size up the situation and maybe make his play.

He took the first hollow that cut off at a right tangent, then lifted the speed of his horse. It was fairly easy going, but his horse was very tired. Yet Kelly crowded it without mercy, for Jim's life was at stake. The interlocking hollows were confusing. Twice he had to pull down, then go on mainly by instinct. The hollows were all dry, cool now, with the morning sun cut off by the hills.

Time was slipping away, and urgency became a hard tension to bear. He grew a little discouraged. Even if he managed to head them off and achieve surprise, he had three men to buck since Jim, by now, had been disarmed. He dogged his way on. Then, when he came to a gully that showed cow tracks, he turned back in toward the valley opening.

Suddenly he came to the end of the gully and stopped his horse. Forward he looked out upon a flat valley floor. To his right he could see trees and structures—the line camp he had expected to be here. Apparently by taking the harder route, he had got ahead of the party. There was no near place to hide his horse, and he feared to take it on with him because it might betray his presence.

Dismounting reluctantly, he left the reins on the animal's neck, turned it about and gave it a slap. As he watched it move back into the hills he had a moment's half-panic. Yet he never considered changing his mind.

He was committed to this effort until Jim was safe or they were both dead.

Hurrying, now, he went on afoot, keeping in against the hills, running for the forward patch of trees and underbrush. This watering place was no spring, he saw as he came nearer. A considerable stream cut across the flat, its banks denuded except where the camp had been built.

He saw as he closed the last distance that there was another sodhouse here and another sod stable. The flat below was still empty, but he was convinced that this was the place the party had been heading. Kelly made his study and his plan. The hut and stable faced each other, their roofs slanting in opposite directions.

Pacing around behind the stable, he sought a way to get up on top. There were pole eaves, but none of them offered a good handhold. A sense of desperation filled him as he stepped into the stable. It was empty but showed fresh horse droppings. This camp had not yet been set up for winter, but for some other purpose it was being used plenty.

He saw an old catch rope and, stepping out with it, threw a loop over one of the longer, higher front eave poles. He went up hand over hand, then pulled the rope up and untied and concealed it behind him. Afterward he lay on the flat roof, panting.

Then he saw the men he had followed, pulling onto the flat, coming his way. He felt his throat tighten, his whole body come alert, the strength of pure fury rushing into it. Then they were cut off by intervening brush. In that interval he slid back a little on the roof, fearing to betray his presence. The sun that burned on his back was getting hotter all the time.

He heard the party riding into the camp, making enough noise though nobody was talking. Kelly's gun was in his hand by then, its grip clutched tight. His breath ran fast and shallow, and he wished that Jim knew he was up here. Then he heard the *screak* of hinges, which meant the soddy door had been opened.

"Inside, blast you," a man said harshly.

Kelly fought down his impulse to pitch into it, heedlessly and blindly. He heard a blur of voices, without understanding what was said, but he judged that they had all gone into the sodhouse. He debated his best course, whether to pull to the edge of the roof and throw down on them when they emerged or to wait. In a moment he was glad he had delayed, for they had not all gone in. He heard a man speak just below him.

"What happened to that old rope that was in here, Spence?" somebody said inside the stable.

Kelly's breathing stopped as he waited to see if they would get suspicious.

"It was there the other day," another voice answered.

"Well, it ain't now. We'll have to hog-tie the cuss with my catch rope, I reckon. Only it's too good a rope to throw into that boghole."

A queer aversion quivered along Kelly's nerves at that. Boghole? The answer to that and a deeper mystery crashed into his mind. It shook and sickened him as he lay there, as yet helpless to act. This was quicksand country. Many of the streams, he knew, were fatally treacherous with it.

That was where the vanished men had gone, where Jim was headed, where Abbie might have wound up except for the spunk that had helped her drive the killers off. Outrage ran through him, and his eyes narrowed to sweaty slits.

The man who had answered to the name of Spence

116

was still talking. "Well, somebody's got to stay here with the bugger till we can fetch the Kilrain filly and Tansy Wooden. We can bring some more old rope, then."

"You think more of a piece of rope than a human life, don't you?"

"Depends on whose rope and whose life it is."

"Well, we better get rid of this one bugger right now and not take chances."

"You heard what Rio said about not doing anything we can't undo till we're sure we can do it all. He's jittery about Chance Comber, and I don't blame him. That little goateed son is hell on wheels in action." The voice faded out.

The mention of Rio Bell's name had surprised Kelly only in that the man seemed to be having the say in this thing. If Rio knew his men had nailed Jim Oliphant, then Jim's life was in double jeopardy. Kelly gave his mind to swift and furious thinking. If they were going to leave Jim here under guard, that was his best chance. Tansy and Colorado were already warned of the lingering danger they had to meet. So Kelly lay there, sweat leaking from his whole body under the bald and burning sun. But he dared not even change position.

It seemed a long while before he heard horses pound out from the line camp, going back the way they had come. Kelly used the cover of the noisy hoofs to squirm back to the rear edge of the roof and drop to the ground. Still holding tight to his gun, he prowled to the stable's back corner and rounded it, pressing close to the earth end wall.

The soddy door was closed, but there was a window in the front wall, too dirty for him to see anything inside. His fear was that someone within might see him.

Yet he could not close the distance between without exposing himself. Pulling in a deep breath, alert in every sense, he prowled on, slow and silent as he could make it. He was almost dizzy with tension when finally he had the solid end wall of the hut beside him.

He had seen in crossing the open that there were still two horses tied to a pole of the corral. One was Jim's own saddler, the first actual confirmation of the prisoner's identity. The other horses had by then pulled out of hearing.

Kelly went on around the back of the sodhouse, wanting to come up on the door from the side that had no window. The walls were too thick for him to hear anything inside, if anything was being said. Then he rounded the other end, moved at once to the front, and kept on, heading for the door.

For the first time he heard voices. Jim was speaking hotly, savagely.

"I always knowed what a polecat you are, Durnbo. I'd sure like to match my one gun against them two hoglegs you tote. But you don't believe in givin' a man any kind of a break, do you?"

"Not if I can help it," Trench Durnbo said and he laughed.

"That tin badge you're wearin'," Jim hooted. "If you had halfways the decency of a white man, you'd take it off before you come out on a job like this. But it pleases your vanity. Makes you feel you're the law that you're really scared of."

Kelly knew that Jim was trying to goad his guard into a reckless attack. It made the cover Kelly wanted. Slowly he lifted the door latch, then he kicked open the door, instantly following its swing.

His gun covered Trench Durnbo before the man knew

what had happened. Amazement leaped into the face of Durnbo as he pulled straight in the chair he occupied. He had a gun on his lap, with which he had been covering his captive, who sat on the edge of the bunk. Durnbo wanted to use it, wanted desperately to swing it on Kelly. His shoulders tightened, but they relaxed without his having moved.

Kelly heard Jim's slowly released breath.

"Sit right tight, Trench," Kelly warned. "Jim, get that gun and the one on his hip."

"Dunno where you come from," Jim gasped, "but, man, you're sure welcome."

He took Durnbo's weapons, one of which he shoved with satisfaction into his own empty holster.

"This," he announced, "is apt to be a shock to Mister Rio Bell."

"Whose ranch did they take you to?" Kelly asked him.

"Comber's Horse Track. But he wasn't home. Durnbo's runnin' this show, and he gave the orders."

"You still working for Comber?" Kelly asked Durnbo. "Or is it against him, now that you've teamed with Rio?"

"That's none of your damned business."

"Then we'll see who squirms the worst when we turn you over to a U. S. Marshal. You been engagin' in a little open claim jumpin', finally, whether you aimed to or not. Finally we can prove it on you."

Trench Durnbo's eyes showed streaks of deep fear, mixed with seething hatred.

"You keep your gun on him, Jim," Kelly said. "Shoot him if he gives you any kind of excuse. But not to kill. We want Trench in shape to talk long and earnest when the time comes. I've got to see if I can pick up my cayuse."

Knowing Durnbo would never get away from Jim, after what the gangling man had experienced at his hands, Kelly went out to where the two horses stood in complete indifference to human passions. Mounting, he rode down the flat to the ravine where he had turned his mount loose. He found it only a short distance up the gully, halted and grazing. Catching it, Kelly turned back for the camp.

CHAPTER 13

THE QUICKSAND SINK, UGLY AND SINISTER IN THE SUN, was some two hundred yards down the sluggish, yellow stream from the line camp. A barbed wire fence around it showed that in the past it had bogged a lot of steers. Kelly stared down at it from the saddle, his eyes dark with his bitter thoughts. Between him and Jim, Durnbo sat his horse in sullen submission.

"Down there somewheres," Kelly muttered, "is evidence enough to get more than one man hanged. I don't reckon it could ever be fished up, but we don't need to, Jim. That's where you were headed, and it ought to pin the deadwood on 'em."

Jim shot a withering stare at Durnbo. "It's where I'd like to send you, alive and kickin'. Hanging is too damned good for you and your stripe."

"Look," Durnbo said urgently, "you boys come up from Texas, the same as me. You got no real stake in this country. Why don't you listen to reason?"

"What kind of reason?" Kelly retorted.

"You can make a lot of money you won't make the way you're heading."

120

"And you can cut out that drivel right now," Jim snapped.

"Let him talk," Kelly rejoined. "I'm sort of interested."

Durnbo didn't take that for a gain, but he was eager to make his offer. For an instant he stared at Kelly. He said, "I could make this thing worth plenty to you boys. If you'd just forget this and let me go. The thing's bigger than a lot of people know."

"I'm ahead of you there," Kelly said. "Rio Bell's out for himself, and it's no bigger than I already suspected."

"He sure is," Durnbo said eagerly, hope beginning to twist through the despair on his shabby features. "Chance Comber don't know it yet, but me and Rio control his crew through the new hands Comber picked up in Ogallala. Men he let me hire."

"And when you got here," Jim said dryly, "you sold out to a higher bidder."

"It happens," Durnbo answered, "that I knowed Rio real well in the old days. It was natural we should team up here. And you boys ought to be on our side instead of bucking us."

"If we ought," Kelly encouraged, "where are the profits?"

"Rio's making himself a good thing outta what the nesters have been doing to Horse Track. Comber's in a tight and knows it. When it pinches hard enough, Rio's going to demand a pardnership in Horse Track as the price of fishing him out. That's why he's turning the heat on the nesters hisself. To get things boiling real good. Comber's tough and mean. But when he discovers he ain't got any gun crew to back his hand, he'll truckle."

"And when Rio gets a say in the ranch," Kelly prodded, "I suppose it will really grow."

121

"It sure will. That nester colony will find out it's been on a picnic up to then. So will some of the other big outfits that have been stringin' with Comber. And Rio ain't going to forget the boys that helped him cut in, anymore than he'll forget the ones that give him trouble."

"But Rio hasn't cut it yet," Kelly murmured, "and won't with you in the hands of a marshal."

"So you're stubborn."

"Just something you wouldn't understand, Trench. We're men instead of reptiles. Come on. Let's get riding."

Not daring to risk running into the same Horse Track riders or any others, Kelly led them out of the little valley at once, entering the concealing, tangled hollows of the sand hills. Kelly remained in the lead, Jim following Durnbo and looking plenty willing to use the gun in his hand if he got the excuse. The horses were all too tired to make fast time. The autumn sun was bright in a cloudless sky.

Kelly figured the best place to take Durnbo now was Badger's Running Iron headquarters. It looked to him like it would be a good idea to muster all the other nesters, both for strength against the showdown they now could crowd and for defense of those either Comber or Rio had marked for immediate death. Yet he didn't know how wise it would be to bring Jim and Linda together. Maybe that should be avoided, if possible.

It took several hours of puzzled, probing riding before they came out into the coulee that Kelly recognized as Horse Track's south line camp. They turned east and very shortly reached Spearhead, his own piece of this broad range.

They watered their horses and let them rest for a

while, never once giving Durnbo the slightest freedom of movement.

Then Kelly said, "Jim, if you ride due south of here, you'll come to Abbie's. They might of had more trouble already, and mebbe Tansy Wooden did too. If not, you better have Tansy come over to Abbie's and hole up there with you and Colorado. We got that dead man and the Horse Track cayuse to go with Durnbo when we bring in the marshal. When them devils find out we've got Durnbo, they'll be plenty rambunctious. I'll take them to Badger's, which'll split their problem for them."

"Sure you can handle him alone?" Jim asked.

Kelly grinned. "When it comes to Durnbo, I got the same itchy fingers you have."

Listening, Durnbo scowled. He was apathetic again but obviously had not given up all hope. He had shown in his talk how impressed he was by Rio Bell's capabilities. He was relying on them now to rescue him from this predicament.

Jim left, mounting the rim and heading south. Riding close behind Durnbo, Kelly followed, but on the bench he cut a slant to the southeast. He had no trouble between there and the edge of the big, hollow saucer nesting the headquarters of Running Iron.

As he rode closer with his prisoner, Kelly saw a familiar figure appear in the doorway of the house. Badger still had his bad arm in a sling, and when he recognized the oncomers he let out a yell.

"What in blue blazes have you got there?"

"Company I'm getting tired of," Kelly answered as he came up. "And let me ask you one. Have you got a manproof hole in the ground anywhere around here? This is Rio Bell's deputy and head gunman, and I aim to hold onto him."

"Taking a deputy prisoner," Badger reflected, "is something I never done yet. Not that I ain't for the idea. There's my meat cooler in the stable. If it keeps out the coyotes, it ought to hold one in." Without waiting for a further explanation, he headed for the soddy barn.

He had walled off a corner of the barn, Kelly discovered, using the same sod blocks that formed the outside walls. There was a solid door and no windows.

"That do?" Badger asked.

"Fine," Kelly agreed.

Durnbo scowled furiously when he was forced into the darkness of the cooler, but Kelly's gun and narrowed eyes decided him to obey orders. When Kelly had shut the door on the man, Badger hasped the padlock and snapped it shut.

"That'll hold him, which is more than I can do with my curiosity. What in tunket's been going on?"

Kelly explained all that had happened since he had last seen Badger, watching the nester leader's features tighten and grow scowling dark. "Well, with Bell coming into the game with steam up, I reckon it's time we called in Uncle Sam."

"Take a while to get a man to the land office and persuade 'em to act," Kelly said. "Meanwhile, we're mighty apt to have to prove our ability to hold onto Durnbo and the evidence over at Abbie's. You better call in some of the nesters who ain't got families to worry about. We're more than likely to need help."

"I expect you're right."

"And it looks like that business is all up to you, since I don't know my way around. Can that shoulder stand much riding yet?"

"It's going to get some whether it likes it or not," Badger said.

"I'll saddle your cayuse."

"That I'd appreciate."

Kelly didn't see Linda until Badger had hoisted himself into the saddle and ridden out. She came to the door as Kelly walked toward the house. She looked better than she had the last time, he saw her. Maybe old Badger had been good for her.

He had a sudden uncertainty as to how much he should tell her of Rio's part in the deadly operations under way in the country. He had always felt that she knew much more about them, already than he did, that this had been a part of her deep unhappiness with Rio.

"Where's Badger going?" Linda asked uneasily.

"Just a little errand," Kelly said. "What's more important is whether there's anything on the stove. I missed my breakfast, and from the looks of that sun I mebbe postponed my dinner, too."

"Come in."

"Where's Jimmy?"

"Having his nap in the bedroom."

Somberly, he said, "There might be trouble here, Linda. Did you see the man I brought in?"

"Yes."

"Recognize him?"

"No."

"Well, he's the man Rio made his deputy. An outright killer from down south."

She had moved to the stove, but she swung toward him, startled. "Have you had more trouble with Rio?"

"Not yet. But this man was one of a tough bunch that had latched onto Jim. They'd of done away with him if I hadn't got there in time. Not because of you. It was over another matter."

"Is—is Jim all right?"

125

"If not fat, he's still plenty sassy. I nearly brought him here, Linda, then decided not to."

"Oh, don't!" she cried.

Quietly, insistently, he said, "Would you consider going back to him?"

"I couldn't. Once is enough to bring uncleanness into Jim Oliphant's life."

"You can't both have Jimmy."

"You don't have to tell me. And it's my place to give him up. I was weak when I let you bring me out here. I've got to go back!"

"You can't!" Kelly thundered. "That man's a cold blooded murderer, Linda!"

"It doesn't make any difference that I found that out too late."

He was moved by the enormous weight of guilt that crushed her spirit. In having once been faithless, she had developed an obsessive idea that she must never weaken or waver again. This was compelling from her a stubborn loyalty to the man for whom she had run away from Jim. It was a kind of punishment, maybe, imposed by her conscience. Yet he knew of nothing to say that might help her think straighter.

There were pots on the stove, and Linda freshened the fire to heat them. She already seemed at home, knew where to find things and worked with efficient ease. She had always been a good homemaker, he remembered. A good mother and wife until the wrong man had come along. He knew she didn't want to talk about her problem, and Kelly didn't press it.

He ate the meal she set on the table for him and, smoking a cigarette afterward, he began to feel the toll that another sleepless night and another tense experience had taken. Yet he dared not sleep, and he drank more coffee. Badger had a lot of riding to do and couldn't possibly be back for hours yet, certainly not before dark . . .

He was not aware that he had dozed, his head canted over in his chair at the table, until he opened his eyes with a bewildering sense of the room's having grown darker. An instant alarm bolted through him at the quietness of the place. Linda wasn't in the room, and he thought of Trench Durnbo.

Had she freed the man in her dogged loyalty to Rio Bell? He was on his feet in the same instant the thought came to him. Then he saw her seated on the doorstep in front. Jimmy was playing in the yard, and she was making him keep quiet while Kelly napped. Just the same, he wasn't sure that Durnbo was still over in the cooler. He felt too guilty to ask her about him, but he had to make sure.

Stepping onto the porch, he said, "By gum, that sure sneaked up on me."

"Feel better?"

"A lot. And I better make sure our man's still cooling over there with Badger's beef. He's weasel enough he could dig his way out under the wall."

She knew that he distrusted her a little; he could see that in her eyes. But she said nothing. He walked on to the barn. The cooler door was still locked, the key was still in his pocket.

He rattled the lock. "Hey, Trench!" he called.

"Yeah?" answered Durnbo's voice.

Embarrassment washed through Kelly. How was Linda ever going to trust herself again if nobody else ever did?

"Need anything?" he called to Durnbo.

"You could let a man have some drinking water."

Kelly was willing to grant the request, but he took care when he opened the door and placed the water bucket inside. Whatever intentions Durnbo might have had, he gave them up. He didn't wheedle any more or try to bargain. He was waiting now for his confederates to move on his behalf, not out of any love for him but because, in the wrong hands, he was a deadly danger to them. Durnbo knew all the angles to a situation like this one.

Kelly was halfway back to the house when he wheeled around. Sound had slid down the slope to the house, that of hoofs hitting hard and fast. Kelly swung again and ran on to the door of the sodhouse.

Sweeping a last glance up the dulling light of the slope, he saw four horses plunging down upon the place. It could be nesters, sent in by Badger, but maybe not. He dared to take no chances. A moment later, when there had been no reassuring hallo, he pulled his gun.

"What is it, Kelly?" Linda said worriedly behind him.

"Not sure. But it ain't got the earmarks of a social call. Mebbe they found out I latched onto Durnbo and tracked me here. Whatever, I don't want 'em to catch sight of you or Jimmy. Hide in the bedroom."

Linda was frightened, more so than she would have been in the old days. He wondered why she had changed so much just because she had loved and lived with the wrong man.

The riders were all strange to him, as were the horses. That didn't mean much. In Ogallala Comber had hired men Kelly had never seen and they usually liked to furnish their own horseflesh. He was determined, then, not to let them come in as they were bent on doing. He

128

fired a shot over their heads to let them know how he felt. The crack of the pistol, as it punched through the beat of hoofs, scattered them. Kelly's lips pinched angrily.

A couple of them had cut in so that the barn concealed them. The other pair went the opposite way and soon had a brush patch between them and the house. Kelly looked around and then saw Badger's rifle in a corner. Dashing over, he picked it up and brought it back to the doorway. Linda and Jimmy had vanished into the bedroom.

"It's bound to be a tussle," he called to her. "But there's a chance Badger or somebody will get here in time." He wished he could feel half the assurance he tried to impart.

The silence that followed was long and bleak. The obstructions kept him from seeing a thing of the hostile visitors. Kelly could hear the crashing of his own blood, then something else, though faintly.

The sod walls of the barn did the muffling, but it was Trench Durnbo calling urgently.

"Boys—boys—I'm in the barn! Get me outta here!"

Weakness hit Kelly's knees for a second. That told them definitely that Durnbo was here. There was a back window in the barn, he remembered. Somebody could crawl through and release Durnbo, because Kelly could not see the cooler door from his position, the only one from which he could fight.

He would have to make a rush for the barn before it was too late, leaving Linda and Jimmy alone in the house.

CHAPTER 14

FOR A SECOND OR SO DESPERATION HELD KELLY STILL. There were two doors to Badger's house, front and rear, and two of the attackers had moved around there. If they cared to they could come in the back. But they wanted Durnbo and must have heard him calling to them. They would be concentrating on getting him into their own hands.

He called, "Linda, I'm scared you're going to have to look out for yourself. If I don't get over to the barn, they'll have Durnbo sure."

She appeared at once, still white in her fear. He handed her the rifle, saying, "You know how to use it."

"Yes."

"Just see nobody gets in here, and you'll be all right."

He pulled the door shut after him as he stepped out. Sucking in a long breath, he made his dash for the barn doorway. Nothing happened, so they were still getting into position for a fight. He was breathing hard when he reached the barn's dusky interior. Well back, where he could watch both front and rear, he halted. The first challenging shot rang out, from behind the barn.

Durnbo still made his desperate plea: "Boys— boys—!"

Kelly saw the glass leave the soddy's one window and knew he had to draw the fire to himself. He got his chance as he swung to look at the back window of the barn. A hat appeared there, a test probably, but he shot. The hat disappeared, but they knew now that there as somebody in here they had to beat.

130

That took the pressure off of Linda and increased his faint hope of holding out until help could come, which seemed to be the best he could do. They would not be apt to know that Badger was away from home. Having to allow for a man in the house, too, they probably would not molest it, centering their attention upon the barn where their man was held prisoner.

For the next few minutes, silence clamped tight about the place. Nobody tried the back window again. The only way they could get into the stable now was by the front, exposed not only to the interior of the barn but to the sodhouse's front door. Kelly could feel sweat rising in his pores as he waited tensely. Then Durnbo was yelling again, almost crying in his hope. He seemed to appreciate that his cronies had a tough nut to crack, that time could easily run out for them.

Then somebody had got around where he could fire on a slant into the barn's interior, through the front door. The shot set off a whole volley at the back of the barn and now from this new angle in front. Kelly saw a bullet tear the corner out of a sodblock at the edge of the door. They were closing in on him.

Suddenly he heard the crash of a rifle. The only one he knew of at the site was the one he had handed Linda, and it came from that direction. He exposed himself enough to sweep a glance at the house. The front door was still shut, but his flesh turned cold. Somebody would be trying for the back door, surely. An attempt to get back to help her now would cost his life.

He cursed bitterly, helplessly to himself. The rifle didn't shoot again, so maybe she had discouraged the aggressor. But now he was afraid to fight a defensive battle, hoping for help. He moved closer to the front opening, determined to spot the man on the oblique angle to the front and eliminate him.

He tried the old trick one of the attackers had used, holding his hat out so that a little of it showed. A pistol cracked instantly, and the hat sailed from his hand. He needed something better, yet knew it just wasn't in the situation for him. He waited through long and bitter moments, and then he heard Linda's scream.

It nearly drove him heedlessly into the open. There was that one woman's outcry, but no more. Then blessedly he heard the beat of rushing hoofs again. He hardly dared to believe it, but somebody was driving in. Suddenly there was shooting from the distance.

Close at hand a man called urgently.

"That's all, boys! Ride!"

"Don't leave me!" Durnbo screamed.

Close by, horses suddenly beat into motion and whipped away. The gun chatter out there brisked and then receded. Kelly grinned, weak, almost hilarious with relief. The attackers finally were getting a little better than they could send. The running fight quickly pulled off into the distance. Suddenly the shooting stopped.

It was Badger and three others who raced into the yard. But by then Kelly was on his way to the house. As he shoved open the door and boiled through, he saw Linda stretched on the floor by the rear door, which was open. The rifle lay on the floor, well away from her. Rushing forward, he could see no sign of bleeding. Then he saw that she had been hit across the side of the head by something, probably the rifle.

She had been tricked somehow, and a terrible fear rose in Kelly. Rushing to the bedroom door, he looked in. Sickness lifted from his stomach to his throat. Jimmy wasn't there. He wasn't in the house anywhere. They had taken him.

Badger had come through the front door. He stared at the limp girl on the floor.

He gasped, "What the hell?"

"They took Jimmy!" Kelly said in a low, thin voice. "Mebbe it was the whole caper, with me thinkin' it was Durnbo they wanted!"

"Well, right now," said Badger, his cheeks whitening, "we got a girl hurt bad."

Linda was deep in unconsciousness, her breath slow and shallow. Kelly lifted her into his arms, and as the burden of her filled them a deep and aged feeling washed through his flesh. Holding her thus for brief seconds before he rose, he thought: It was always her . . . there wasn't ever any more . . . Shaken, bewildered, he carried her to the bed. The years, and all that they had held, seemed to fall from him and Linda. I loved her then, he thought, but because Jim was so close a friend, I wouldn't let myself admit it . . .

"We got to get her a doctor," he choked to Badger.

The patriarch went out. A moment later a horse left at a clatter. Kelly searched his mind desperately, trying to think what he could do for Linda until more skilled help could come. There wasn't a thing, he realized, but to make her comfortable as possible and keep her warm.

"Don't blame yourself," Badger was saying at his elbow. "I'd have figured they were after Durnbo, the same way you did."

So deep was his preoccupation, Kelly hadn't even heard the man come in. Jarred out of his lost memories, Kelly straightened and went to the back door. It did not take him long to figure out what must have happened there. Linda's first shot had been to drive somebody off. But the man had been crafty enough to sneak in from the side and get against the back wall. He must have made some small disturbance. The instant she poked her rifle out, he had grabbed and wrested it from her. Then had come that vicious blow with the weapon, and Jimmy had been in his hands.

Badger introduced the two men who had remained with him. "These boys are Pete Akers and Nick Croner, Kelly. We come a-hikin' but it just wasn't fast enough."

"And we got us a pretty kettle of fish," Kelly said harshly. "We don't even know who was back of takin' Jimmy, and I see too late what a smart stroke it was. We can't send for any marshal. We don't dare do a thing with Durnbo or that Horse Track cayuse I latched onto."

"If it was Chance Comber," Badger added grimly, "he could even get a quit-claim to Spearhead outta you."

"He could in a minute," Kelly agreed.

"Well, all we can do is wait for their next move. Which they might not make for a long while. They got us helpless. They can just about get away with anything."

"Not if I can find Jimmy."

"Don't even think of that," Badger rapped. "Comber or Bell—either one would kill that button in a minute if we crowded."

Dismally, Kelly had to agree. He was physically sick from the portent that had opened up since the instant when he had seen those men whipping down on the place. The thing might yet cost Linda's life and even Jimmy's, while there wasn't a thing that could be done about it.

Badger was building a fire in the kitchen stove, starting a new pot of coffee, but his face looked a hundred years old. Akers and Croner had been looking around and came in to report that the thing had been without cost to the attackers, there being no sign of blood spilled anywhere. That was no surprise to Kelly. They'd had every advantage, in every way.

Darkness came on while Badger cooked supper. Kelly had no wish to eat with the others, but they forced him to try it and he downed a little food. It didn't make him feel any better.

Afterward, as they sat in the lamplight, Badger said, "Well, we'll go ahead and stand guard over Durnbo, anyhow. If they get him back, we can at least make him cost them Jimmy. You want to take the first watch, Nick? Then you and Pete handle that. Me and Kelly will watch over little Linda. Damme, it's going to be awful when she comes to, if she does, and we have to tell her about her boy."

It was a relief to Kelly to be alone with Badger and the motionless Linda.

"She's a good girl," he said brokenly to the older man. "And I sure wish Jim was here."

"Whyn't you go and fetch him?"

"He wouldn't come."

"Why don't you try?"

Kelly knew he was going to do that, make his try. It probably wouldn't help the unconscious girl a whit, and it would be like taking a mauling to tell Jim what had happened to his son. But even as he considered that, Kelly was on his way to get a horse.

Disdaining the dangers that the night might hold for him, he rode swiftly westward, growing familiar with the country now and losing no time. Yet it seemed a long while before he saw ahead of him the yellow glow of Abbie's lamp.

He hailed the house as he descended the slope. The door came open, and he saw it was Jim who stood there as he whipped in.

"What's the trouble?" Jim called.

"Jim—they got Jimmy!"

"What's that?"

"They hit the place with just me and Linda and him there," Kelly panted. "I figured they wanted Durnbo. But from the slick way they worked it, they were after Jimmy all along."

"Bell," Jim breathed. "Goddam his black soul to hell."

"It could as well have been Comber, Jimmy's priceless to either man. Jim, Linda's hurt bad. I wish you'd come to her now."

For a long moment Jim was silent.

"She never sent you."

"No," Kelly admitted. "But mebbe you could do her some good. Jim, we rode a lot of trails together. All three of us. I'm asking you to come."

"All right," Jim said and stepped back into the house. When he reappeared he wore his hat and gunbelt. He started toward the corral.

Abbie slipped out quietly then. "Could I help any, Kelly?" she asked.

"I don't reckon so, Abbie. We already sent for a doctor. I just figured mebbe if Jim could swallow his pride—"

"It isn't his pride," Abbie cut in. "Jim's too big for that. He just doesn't believe that Linda's got over her love for Bell. You can't blame him for steering clear of her, can you?"

"I guess not."

"And don't blame yourself so, Kelly. I know you well enough to know you did your best."

"Where's Colorado?"

"Asleep. We'll be all right."

Then Jim was riding toward Kelly. Turning his

136

horse, Kelly rode out into the night with his old saddlemate.

His thoughts went back as they traveled. Once they hadn't known which of them would get Linda, if either ever would, and it hadn't made any difference between them. That was why he felt everything that Jim was feeling now, why he would give his life gladly if he could undo what had happened, maybe out of his own failure.

He knew now what Linda had been feeling, even before the new disaster. He had come up against something greater than he was, something he couldn't help, discovering his own weakness and limitation and the fact that he was less than the hell-on-wheels he had once believed himself to be. He could be outsmarted, he could be beaten, and he was a more humble man as he rode with Jim.

When they reached Running Iron, they were still well ahead of the time when the doctor could be expected to arrive. Badger looked up from his place beside Linda's bed when the two men stepped into the room. His face showed relief.

Then Jim Oliphant was looking down at his unconscious wife.

Kelly had never expected it to come this way. Jim dropped to his knees beside the bed. He found one of her hands. Softly he said, "Linda—little Linda—" Badger rose, and he and Kelly went outside.

It was around midnight when the doctor got there, riding a saddle horse and accompanied by the nester who had gone for him. The men still waited outdoors; they did not follow the medico in. Stillness again pressed upon the place, the quietude of death and of mute prayer.

It seemed a long while before Jim came out. "Well, I guess she'll make it," he said.

"You tell her about the boy?" Kelly asked.

"Not yet." Then Jim's harsh voice softened. "But she knew me. She—she looked glad to see me there."

Jim was heading for the corral, apparently to get his horse. Kelly followed, a sudden intuition squirming in him. Coming up with Jim, he said, "Don't try it, Jim. I know how you feel. But it would only make Jimmy's chances poorer if you do anything."

"I should have killed that man, Kelly."

"And so should I. But we ain't built that way, Jim. God help us, we got to carry the burden of being civilized."

"What can we do, then?"

"Just wait," Kelly said on a long sigh. "Wait and see what their price'll be. Then pay it." Kelly put his hand on Jim's shoulder. "And after we've paid it and Jimmy's safe, you and me are going to forget we're civilized."

Jim came back to the soddy steps with him, where the other anxious men waited. But nobody bothered him, not wanting to intrude upon his awful tragedy.

Then the doctor came to the doorway, saying quietly, "She wants to see you both, Jim and Kelly, she said. She knows what's happened. She understood it even before that man hit her."

Kelly hated to follow Jim in, but since it was Linda's desire he did. In the yellow lamplight, she lay awake, yet as motionless as if she were still unconscious. Kelly swallowed. He felt uncertain, lost, numbed. She looked up, seeing him first.

"They got Jimmy away from me."

"It wasn't your fault. They fooled me even worse than you."

"It was my fault. I know too much about Rio now,

138

not too little. He hates Jimmy. He threatened to kill him if I ever spoke out or acted against him. Now he's got him, and I've got to go back to him."

"That's not what he wants now," Kelly told her. "We don't even know but what those men were acting on Comber's orders."

Linda looked at her husband. "Jim, I'm awfully sorry. For—everything."

Jim shifted his weight. He didn't look at her. "We got to think of him now. We'll do what we have to."

"You don't think they'll kill him?"

"Not if we don't force their hand."

She eased a little and afterward seemed to sleep. Kelly could not tell from Jim's face whether the man still loved her or had been brought here by love of his son and hatred of the man who had broken up their home.

At that inopportune moment his own deep love of Linda rose up in Kelly, taunting and accusing him. There followed a clarity such as he had never known. The very first mistake might have been his own.

Had he competed with Jim, regardless of their close friendship, none of this might have happened. Without vanity, he realized that in him Linda could have found satisfaction for her own restless nature, so that she would never have been drawn to Rio Bell.

Too late . . . too late . . . why were those words so often the cry of the human spirit when, finally, wisdom had come?

By morning the doctor pronounced Linda out of danger, and he rode out for town. Badger had asked him not to report the violence and explained why. Maybe Rio Bell knew all about it, already, or maybe he didn't know a thing. They dared not take any chance with young Jimmy's life.

The gathered nesters still hung around in impotent fury. Badger cooked a breakfast, and they ate it mechanically. All they could do was wait, wait, wait. God damn them, Kelly thought again and again. It was a long, terrible morning. Linda might have been better off if the blow had killed her outright instead of letting her die by the minute this way.

"By God," Badger bawled finally, "I'm going over to Horse Track and offer whatever Comber wants for that young 'un."

"We don't know it was him," Kelly said doggedly. "But I been thinking. We might be scaring 'em off from getting in touch with us, so many being here. Yet I don't reckon we ought to cut down the guard over Trench, either. So mebbe I better go back to my place and give anybody that wants to a chance to speak his piece."

"You might be right," Badger conceded. "But you ought to have somebody side you."

"That'd spoil it. I'll go alone."

Badger thought that over for a moment.

"Go on," he said.

Kelly got a horse and was soon riding out, his shoulders tightening again. But there wasn't anything he wouldn't give to bring the boy back to Linda. He didn't hesitate a minute.

CHAPTER 15

HE REACHED THE BLUFF ABOVE SPEARHEAD TO SEE A horse tied to the fence in front of the soddy. It wore a Horse Track brand and stood hipshot, as if it had been waiting there a while. Kelly's eyes narrowed, a mixed anger and hope mounting in him. This could be more

140

trouble for him, or it could be the contact he now wanted desperately with the boy's abductors. He rode down to the bottom with extreme care.

As he came around in front of the house, his eyes widened again in a sharp stare. Chance Comber sat in the shade of the building, his back resting against the wall. Now he had no air of hostility about him. Recognizing Kelly, he jumped hastily to his feet.

"I hoped you'd show up pretty soon, Drake," he said, his voice harsh and tight with some driving need within him. "You and me are where we've got to get together, and that's all there is to it."

"You know anything about Jimmy Oliphant?" Kelly rasped.

"I know plenty, and that's why I'm here. Rio Bell directed that caper from my place. His Texas gunhands brung the kid there. Then they left again, taking the young 'un."

"So you're innocent as a new-born lamb!" Kelly hooted.

"You got to believe me. We're in the same tight, and there's no time to lose about it. He laid down the law to me. He's bought my crew and controls it. He's got a hold on your side that's going to bring you to time real quick. I'd need your help, but mebbe I know how we can euchre him."

"You're good at that," Kelly admitted. "As good as Rio is. But I don't see why I should have any dealings with you just because you're caught, finally, where you got to yell for help. I knew you were going to be. I got it out of Durnbo. I could of made my own dicker with you, if I'd been interested."

"Bell's set to take over this whole blasted range!" Comber said desperately.

141

"Sure. And why wouldn't you rather have a half interest in that eventually than my help right now?"

Bitterly, yet truthfully, Comber said, "His talk about a pardnership with me is pure horse sweat. Soon as he was through with me, he'd deal me plumb out."

"If it's got you scared as hell, I'm damned glad of it."

"Look," Comber said, beginning to show a trace of anger. "You ain't going to get a chance to ransom that kid. Rio's in no hurry about that. He knows you can't make a move against him as long as he holds that card. So he figures to have things the way he wants before he begins his dickering with your side."

The impact of that made Kelly close his eyes for an instant. Rio was capable of it, holding the whole nester colony in an agony of apprehension while he perfected his position. Even afterward there was no guarantee that he would return Jimmy unharmed. Linda said he hated the boy, and he probably by now hated Linda.

"All right," Kelly said. "I'm ready to listen. What's your proposition?"

"I think I know where they took that kid. But right now there ain't a man on my spread I'd trust to help me. That's why I come here."

"Trying to rescue that boy would be a good way to get him killed, Comber."

"Not if we work it right, which is where I figured I could help you out."

"What all do you want in return?"

"Nothin' except to get out of Rio Bell's bear trap."

"So what do we do?"

Comber was looking excited now. "It never entered Rio's head I'd throw in with you, and he knows I ain't got any other help. But from the orders he give his men, I

142

caught on to where they aim to keep the young 'un while they wind up the caper. Wouldn't be more than one man or two there with him. They won't be expecting to be jumped. If we could come in on 'em quiet enough, we could probably handle it without much risk to the kid."

Kelly hated the thought of taking any kind of chance with Jimmy's safety. Yet he saw no alternative, now. He had to do it.

"When?" he asked.

"The sooner the better.

"Then let's get riding."

It was a bitter dose having to team up with Comber. Kelly had come to bear an intense loathing of the man. He placed no trust in him, even now with Comber brought at last to his knees. He dreaded to think of some misstep of his own or Comber's that would result in further disaster.

With Comber leading, as he knew the country, they pressed deeper into the hills. The particular region was vacant, or was a remoter part of the winter range Kelly had taken from Horse Track when he seized the water supply. The merciless sun brought sweat to his skin, which mixed with the windswept dust to form an uncomfortable coating on his exposed skin.

They had ridden at a steady, mile-eating gait for some two hours when Comber made a motion to the northeast, where there rose through the haze the rougher outlines of broken hills.

He said, "We're getting close, and we'd best plan it. There's a dinky little spring there, the only water in these parts. From what was said, I had a good notion this was where they'd come. Now, we better hook around east and north. Then we can come in on their camp from a direction they ain't watching so close."

"How far is it?"

"Quarter mile, mebbe. But we better go the long way round."

Even as Comber spoke, Kelly had drawn his gun. His cold eyes drilled into Comber's; there was a contemptuous smile on his lips.

"Not we, Comber. Me. You'd sure admire to have that button in your own hands. I ain't been impressed by your desire to make peace with the nesters. Hands up, now, while I get your hogleg. With your fangs pulled, I don't reckon you'll get in too close to where hostile lead might be flying."

"Why, damn you!" Comber breathed. Yet his smoking eyes convinced Kelly that he had much more in mind than the rescue of a child, even when Bell's power over him would be diminished thereby. What was a trump card for Bell would be one for Chance Comber. But the hard warning in Kelly's eyes made the man lift his arms upright.

Kelly rode in and got the man's pistol, which he shoved under his own belt.

"Now, get out of that saddle," he rapped. "I'm taking no chances on you getting a warning to that camp."

Chance Comber shook with rage as he obeyed. He stood helpless while Kelly started his horse off at a run, back in the direction from which they had come. Then Kelly rode on alone.

The country he entered immediately was sufficiently wind-worn and broken to keep him fairly well concealed from watching points in the roundabout. Yet he had to move with all possible haste, for there was little doubt that Comber would now switch his allegiance the other way, and try to warn the camp he had been equally willing to betray. Soon Kelly had

144

discovered horse tracks that came in from an angling canyon.

They'll take me there, he thought in grim satisfaction.

He dismounted and left his horse in the side gully he had followed in. He took a careful look at his .45, then started on afoot. The first thing he had to accomplish was to get a look at the place and appraise what he'd face at the camp he was now sure he would find.

He moved higher on the slope, onto the shadowed side, and walked quietly. Yet it seemed to him that every step dragged up more sound than a herd of rushing steers. The sand was hot under his boots, the shadow he used insufficient to give him much concealment. He gave a start when a bird cut away above him and swept off against the depthless blue sky.

Quite suddenly he found himself upon a minor top of land and gazing down upon a scene of human activity. He had reached a camp, sure enough. Comber had not been lying about it. Kelly first saw smoke wisping above the distant bottom. His lips ruled into a flat, firm line. He could get a better look from this same side, crossing the ridge, coming abreast, then moving back in.

He slipped on along that course, his caution doubled, the tensions in him subsiding now that he had a concrete picture of what he faced. Yet he had not from the start felt fear for himself, only for the boy. But he was wholly convinced now that Jimmy's welfare would be better served by this than by letting him remain too long in Rio's power.

Working his way along carefully, he was soon where he wanted to be, bellied down and, his hat removed, cautiously peering across the top of the rim at the camp. A cook fire was directly below him, in front of a fly raised on poles. Brush to the left of that disclosed the small spring Comber had mentioned. He could see only one man there and that one quite plainly. There was no sign of Jimmy, if the boy was being allowed to run loose. He was sure the man was one of those he had seen riding down upon Running Iron before the attack.

Kelly began to belly himself inch by inch to the ridge top, then on down making each movement with excruciating slowness and care. But the man below seemed complacent. He wasn't expecting any trouble now.

Then, his mouth dry, his throat tight, Kelly called out.

"Lift your hands, buck! Otherwise, don't twitch a muscle!"

The man's spasmodic reflexes violated that order a trifle. He jerked his head about, started to rise, then saw Kelly and the gun trained on him. His arms shot up. He had a look of complete amazement on his whiskery features.

Kelly was on his feet by then, hurrying on down. He could see a horse in the brush, just one.

"How in hell," the man gasped, "did you ever find this place?"

"Never mind that. Where's the boy?"

"He ain't here."

"Don't lie to me, damn you." Kelly stepped forward, his eyes sudden pits of danger.

The man backed up a step and swallowed.

"The kid bawled himself to sleep. He's over there."

Kelly didn't risk turning his head to look, just then. Stepping in, he took the man's weapon from its holster.

"What you going to do with me?" the fellow bawled.

"Tie you up, mebbe, and let the sun fry your brains out. But mebbe that'd be too easy on you. Turn around."

146

Without mercy, he whipped down with his gun barrel when the man obeyed. The guard let out a grunt, then dropped in a limp fall.

Jimmy was asleep on a blanket under the fly and behind a heap of camping gear. His face was sweaty, dusty, and tears had made runnels of mud under his eyes. Kelly swallowed a bitter curse at the men who had used him this way, then gently shook the boy.

"Jimmy—it's Kelly—your friend."

The boy awakened in alarm, made recognition and let out a cry. His arms came around Kelly's neck and clutched tight.

"Mommy!" he cried desperately. "Where's Mommy?"

"We're going there right now."

Then it was that Kelly heard Comber shouting in the distance. He had walked in close enough to the camp; he figured he could warn it of what was coming. Pulling to a stand, Kelly got the horse in the brush and hastily saddled it. The mount was fresher than his own, which he abandoned when he cut out in the opposite direction with Jimmy riding in front of him.

He had Jimmy, which was the big thing, but he was far from being back home with him. Comber would take his horse when he learned what had happened here, and Comber wasn't on the side of Kelly Drake any longer. He wanted this boy himself, Kelly was sure of it, and he still meant to get him if he could.

Then Kelly heard sound that congealed his blood in cold fear. Horses, and more than one of them, were drawing near along the route he had followed in. That gave him a bleak, belated insight into the guard's complacency when he had come upon the camp. The man had known that some of his cronies were due to

147

arrive at any time. Kelly dug in his spurs then, realizing he had a hard ride ahead of him.

Comber would join them, telling them fully of whom they pursued, some big lie covering his own presence here. He would be with them, rearmed by one of them. Kelly had a sick, hard lump in his stomach.

He gave no thought to direction, now, simply hunted country that would help him stay out of their clutches. Remembering the trip he had made with Badger into the northward region after the cattle, he figured that was as good a place as any to head. The terrain turned into roughs up there, which was a better place for him than these treacherous sand hills.

He could no longer hear anything in the rearward distance. Yet every track that his running horse laid down was an indelible marker on his course. There was nothing in sight he could use to foul his trail. He could only hurry on yet did not dare to press too hard because of the unknown miles this animal might have to carry them.

Silently he cursed the odds against him, fighting down a mounting sense of panic. The wornout Jimmy had relaxed against him, trusting him fully to take him to his mother. Presently Kelly swung the horse on a long slant up the slope of the ridge to the left. He followed the parallel bottom with slightly easier going. But a backward glance showed that same easily followed trail.

For a while, then, he rode a meandering course, crossing ridges, turning back a short distance on his own course, veering off in another direction. The despairing thought hammered in his mind with each hoof beat: They'll never let you make it back.

The country ahead began to show a much greater

roughness. Soon he discerned a prominence that would give him a look at the backtrail. He found a way up, slowed painfully by the pitch. On top he halted for the horse was blowing hard. He let Jimmy down to the ground and swung out of the saddle.

He rolled a cigarette as he stared into the sun-bright distance. At first it was empty of anything except the monotonous roll of tawny hills.

He had smoked half the cigarette when he dropped it in haste and ground it out. Far back, three or four horsemen had topped over a ridge, coming into view then vanishing again. There could be no doubt that they were following his sign, riding hard.

"Thirsty," Jimmy complained.

"We got more riding to do first, pardner. Mebbe a lot of it."

Back in the saddle again hugging Jimmy tight to his body, Kelly pressed on. There wasn't much use now in trying to be deceptive; if he escaped at all it would have to come through speed. The chances of that were far from good for the horse he forked was only mediocre and already showing signs of wear.

He stayed on the bench, riding west. It was empty, primeval, a patch of real estate that had lain here unclaimed through the ages. Beyond it he saw scrubby timber. When he had reached the concealment and shade of the trees, he again halted to rest his horse for a few minutes. Not only his own life, but Jimmy's, depended on its stamina. He kept a close watch on the long, open bench he had just crossed. Far down, well over a mile, he saw horses break up over and into view.

That forced him on, desperately seeking a way he could outwit them. The trees grew larger, denser, and that was an immediate help. But he knew from the very nature of the country that this cover would soon run out. Now he began to watch for a place where he might hide and let them pass on ahead of him.

It was quite a while before he found a place that encouraged him to try that. The trees ran out, but off to his right he suddenly saw something that interested him. He swung the horse that way. A moment later he halted where the bench broke away above a narrow bottom well grown with willows and cottonwood.

That probably meant water, which the horse needed as badly as did Jimmy and himself. It offered more cover for a while. But the drop down the bluff would have discouraged him, even without the boy to consider.

Then his plan came full-blown into his mind.

He rode back from the edge, blood pumping urgently in his ears, and pressed on until he came to a rock patch. There he stopped the horse and swung from the saddle onto the hot top of a rock. He lifted Jimmy over, then using his hat, slapped the horse hard across the rump. It went tearing on.

A backward glance showed Kelly the pursuit still had not emerged from the trees. Carrying Jimmy and jumping from rock to rock, he made his way to the back side of the outcrop without leaving a boot print. Dropping to the ground there, where the tracks were not so apt to be discovered, he ran for the close-by edge of the rim.

It still looked a long way down, but they could make it easier afoot than by trying to take the horse with them. He edged over, holding the boy tightly, and dropped to the first sharp slant below him.

CHAPTER 16

THE UNDERFOOTING WAS DIRT AND ROCK, NAKED OF vegetation. It was all Kelly could do to dig in the edges of his boots and gain a footing. Jimmy's eyes turned large with fear. He clung tighter but did not protest.

"*Bueno hombre*," Kelly praised.

Presently he was at a place where rock broke through the earth surface of the slope. He edged around it carefully and, below it and cut off from the top of the rim, he stopped to catch his breath.

It was only a matter of time until they would overtake the horse, or get close enough to see that it was riderless. Then they would backtrail, and he had no hope that the rock crop where he had dismounted would escape their notice then. All he had gained was time, and he knew little about the vicinity below him. Maybe it would only create another trap.

Then he heard them clatter past above.

At once he took up the dangerous task of getting on down the cliff, impeded by Jimmy but with his safety being the concern that drove Kelly. The remaining descent seemed too much for an unencumbered man even, but he started doggedly on. The surface bulged below him, cutting from sight what lay beyond. The earth under his feet was loose, so that he had to dig in his foot with each careful step.

Then came the one wrong step he had dreaded. Without warning, the soft underfooting gave way, and his feet slipped from under him. He came down hard, absorbing the full shock of the fall to protect the boy. Then they were sliding free and fast over the bulge. He must have fallen ten feet before he hit the earth again, the sharp slant of it lessening the impact. Then he slid on and finally came to a stop. They were down, and Jimmy was unhurt.

"Anyhow, we sure made time," Kelly told the boy.

He had lost skin from his elbows, arms and hip, yet was scarcely aware of it. They were almost at the creek bank, and he rose and ducked quickly into the growth. One look upward showed him an empty rim. Then he went on to the edge of the water. It was a clear stream and looked cold and safe to drink.

He scooped up a handful of water to taste and found it sweet. Then he helped Jimmy flatten out and get a drink. Afterward he satisfied his own clawing thirst. They were deep in the wilds now, he realized, and afoot. That was hazard enough without the men who were trying to catch them. The impulse to keep moving swelled in him. But he knew he had to make some kind of plan before he lost himself even more completely, one that had also to elude the pursuit.

"I'm hungry," Jimmy said, now that his quenched thirst let him realize it. "I want my mommy." More than that, his features showed that he was extremely tired.

The drives in Kelly were getting hard to hold in. From long experience he knew that the best way out of unfamiliar country was to follow downward along any available stream. But if those riders managed to pick their way back here, they would anticipate that effort and try to cut in ahead of him somewhere downstream. That suggested a course upstream as the only one he could take with any hope of escape. Into rougher country, farther away from food and shelter and safety from the elements themselves.

Despair swelled in him, and he was in that moment

152

fully aware of his own spent strength and gnawing hunger. He would have to risk the downward course and his pursuers. Picking Jimmy up again, he lifted him to sit on his shoulders and started on, following the creek and concealed from the bluff top by the brush.

If they got back to the cliff top and saw his boot tracks, as eventually they would, they might hesitate about coming down in fear that he was forted up in the undergrowth. At least that might divide their force, somebody waiting here while somebody investigated the lower country. That would help him a little.

The going proved easier than he had dared to hope, and that pumped energy into him. As he walked steadily, he reviewed as best be could his movements since leaving Spearhead with Comber. He was confident that this stream would eventually take him back into the sand hills, eventually to a settled region. But already the rough walking in high heeled boots had rubbed blisters on his heels. His legs ached. It was increasingly hard to keep Jimmy riding easily on his shoulder.

When Jimmy began to nod up there, Kelly knew he had to stop so they both could rest. He found a place in the shade, still close to the creek, and put the boy down. Jimmy looked around with vacant, groggy eyes. Then his head nodded.

Kelly had no choice but to make him comfortable and let him have his nap, while he himself tried to recruit some of his exhausted strength. The roundabout was wholly quiet except for the amiable brawling of the creek. The stream ran through palisades now, the bluffs fallen behind. That made it less likely that he could be come upon by surprise. He began to feel Jimmy's weighting drowsiness himself.

To fight it, he rolled and lighted a cigarette, which he

found tasteless and flat. Presently he tossed it, half-smoked, into the creek. Beguiling waves of languor began to wash through his brain . . .

He was unaware that any time had passed until he heard a voice behind him rap out.

"A good try, Drake. But not good enough."

A jolting rebellion exploded through Kelly. Then he remembered that he dared not risk a fight with Jimmy here beside him. Slowly he turned his head.

Chance Comber held a pistol on him, a look of high triumph twisting his face out of shape. There was another man with him, a stranger.

"You wanted it this way," Comber taunted. "So don't look so sick."

Kelly could only sit there, playing on them his dull, shocked stare.

"Not much worse off than I'd of been if I had strung with you," he rapped.

"Mebbe not. I want that boy."

"But not me?"

"Yeah," Comber said. "I need you, too. In fact, I got to have you." To the stranger he barked, "Go fetch the other boys."

The puncher might have been one of those who had defected from Comber and gone over to Bell's support. But he looked at the rancher now with new respect, seemed to realize who held the trump card. He nodded and walked off.

"I'm taking that kid," Comber said to Kelly, "and never you mind where. You're going back to Running Iron. Then you're coming over to Horse Track with what I want in exchange for the boy."

"Which is?"

"That Horse Track cayuse you're holding onto. I

don't give a damn about the carcass of the man who was riding it. He was one of Bell's Texans. Then I want from you, Drake, a quit-claim to my line camp."

"How about Trench Durnbo?"

Comber laughed. "Go ahead and turn him over to the marshal. He's Rio's man, as that deputy badge will show, and he's Rio's problem."

Presently three men rode in, leading the horse Kelly had turned loose. They all looked to Comber for orders now. The man had made a tremendous comeback in the last couple of hours.

"Get riding," Comber said to Kelly. "I want you ahead of us."

"I'm not showing up at Horse Track," Kelly blazed. "You'd never let me or Jimmy, either one, get away from there alive. I'll have what you want at Spear—at your line camp. Just you and the boy. That's the only way he'll ever do you any good."

"All right," said Comber, aware that he dared not demand too much because of the uncertainties created by Bell. "It's getting on in the day. But we can both be there by daylight tomorrow. Don't try any more tricks, Drake, if you want to take that kid home to its mother."

Kelly rode out, steeling himself against Jimmy's wailing protests, then his frightened screaming. But the sounds rang in his memory long after he had quit hearing them. He rode doggedly southward, crushed with a renewed sense of defeat, of failure.

He reached Running Iron just as dusk began to thicken over the hills. Everyone present was in the yard to watch him ride in. They all seemed to read from his face the bad news he brought them. He told them what had happened, what he now had to do.

Linda stood with them, although apart from Jim.

Kelly couldn't bear to look at the distress that twisted her face.

"Don't blame yourself," Jim said. "You made a good try, and it's not your fault you ain't got the strength of a bull buffalo. It's something to have the boy in Comber's hands instead of—" Jim didn't finish that thought.

Kelly nodded. "But if he wasn't so worried about Bell, he'd be every bit as bad. We've got to make the swap as soon as we possibly can."

"No."

The voice was a woman's, Linda's. Kelly swung his head to look at her.

"It doesn't make much difference which of them comes out on top," she said dully. "Let either one get in the clear now, and the killing will be worse than ever. I can't ask for my son back at that price." She looked at Jim, then. "You're his father. What do you say?"

"I reckon," Jim said, "that you're right."

"Then defy them," Linda told Kelly.

He stared at the girl in sharp wonder. Even Jim, had he been less disturbed, would have seen how true blue she was.

It was the others present who decided the issue. They were the men whose lives might yet be taken in the struggle that would come if Comber again was free to act as he chose.

"Not by a damned sight," Badger growled. "We get Jimmy back and start from raw?"

The others nodded vigorously.

Kelly forced himself to eat the meal that was ready. He hardly tasted it, but afterward some of the jaded inertia of his body began to leave. Badger had sent somebody over to Abbie's for the Horse Track horse Comber was anxious to get back into his own hands.

156

Kelly, in the lamplight, used Badger's paper, pen and ink to write out the quit-claim that was Comber's other demand. To make certain Comber would accept it, he had it witnessed by Badger and Nick Croner.

"I'll be back with Jimmy," he told Linda before he rode out on a fresh horse of Badger's. "Or I won't be back."

"I know you'll do your best, Kelly," he said. "God help you."

Leading the other horse, he rode north again under the wheeling stars. The fresh mount he forked ate up the distance, yet he was fighting drowsiness again by the time he reached the rim above the camp he was being forced to give up. He had no regrets about that, if only he could get Jimmy safely into his custody again. And he knew one thing. Comber wasn't going to get what he wanted until he had paid the price he had promised to pay.

He left the horses in front of the soddy so that they could be seen readily. He entered the place cautiously but found nothing alarming, no evidence of any disturbance there. He started a fire in the stove and put a pot of coffee on to cook. He knew that he had to sleep soon, and thought he knew a way he could do it safely.

Taking the quit-claim deed from his pocket, he hid it under the coffee in the can. Comber would not molest him until he had it, in his own hands. He stacked other cans on the floor against the door so that, if it was opened, it would make a noise he would hear. He placed a chair where it could not be seen from the window. He sat down.

He had long since learned the trick of setting his mind to wake up when he wanted. When he did so, his neck was stiff and the fire was out. Crossing to the window, he saw by the position of the stars that it was not far from dawn. He started up the fire again, and when he had drunk a cup of coffee he felt fairly well restored. He went ahead and fixed himself a breakfast.

He was watching when, at daylight, he saw a rider coming up the long flat of the bottom. He soon realized that it was Chance Comber. From the bulk of the figures, he felt pretty sure the man had brought the boy. Kelly met him at the fence.

Comber looked at the Horse Track animal with satisfaction. It was evidence that he had won his game. Without a greeting, he said, "You wrote up that quit-claim yet?"

"First, hand me that boy."

The man's willingness to obey, Kelly figured, would tell him whether Comber had sent help sneaking in ahead of him to get stationed somewhere close. But Comber's eyes hardened.

"Not much. I don't figure to double-cross you, Drake. But I don't figure to give you a second chance at me."

Comber seemed to be acting in good faith, though only out of strict necessity.

"All right," Kelly said. He handed Comber the quit-claim he had written in Badger's house. He saw a smile on Comber's face as he examined it and saw that Badger himself had witnessed the instrument. Then Comber handed Jimmy over. He seemed anxious to get away from there.

"I brought wire cutters," Comber said. Reaching into a saddle pocket he got them out. "Open that fence and fetch my horse out and I'll be gone."

Kelly obeyed, ready to kill the man at the first sign of treachery. But when he handed up the reins of the Horse Track horse, the man was so pleased with his progress he looked almost amiable.

"It might interest you to know," Comber said with

158

satisfaction, "that Rio Bell don't know yet he's had the rug jerked out from under him. My men are backing me again, and we sent the others packin'."

"All you're out," Kelly said bitterly, "is having your own sheriff in office."

"That's about it," Comber agreed. He swung his horse about and left.

"You poor little coot," Kelly told the boy. "This time you're really going home to your ma and pa."

Yet he stopped on the rim to look down once more at the place he had owned legitimately for a short period of time. It would have been fine to have held onto it. Its loss showed him how much he had banked on staying in this country, of finding a way of life that would be permanent and—yes, and not alone. It was gone now, and every other gain they had made against Comber and Bell.

But he had Jimmy Oliphant safe in his arms.

Again they waited for him as he rode in to Badger's little headquarters. But his reassuring shout from the distance had told them he had made the exchange successfully. Linda came running forward to take the boy and hold him tight.

The eyes that looked up to Kelly were bright with grateful tears. She hurried inside with her precious burden. Jim turned after her, but nobody else followed.

CHAPTER 17

AS HE CAME DOWN THE SLANT TOWARD RUNNING IRON headquarters, Rio Bell rode openly. Nick Croner saw him first and let out a whoop.

"Boys—here comes our John Law and soul alone!"

The four men sitting on Badger's front steps shoved

to their feet. It was by then midmorning, and they had been planning the defense they would now have to make against Horse Track. Comber had made it clear that he would press the attack on the nester colony even harder than before.

Staring out at the approaching rider, Kelly had a queasy feeling in his middle. It was an incredible act of daring for Rio to come here alone—unless he relied upon the power and prestige of the star he wore so brazenly. The man's face was a mask as he rode into the ranchyard. His mouth was still puffed from the fight in the Longhorn. When he spoke, he showed missing teeth.

Laying a blunt stare on Badger, Rio said, "I hear you're holding Trench Durnbo here. I want him."

"So?" Badger said, and his gaunt shoulders pulled back. "Official or otherwise?"

"Official," Rio snapped. "You got no right to hold him."

"And you got no official right to turn him loose."

"I got plenty of right to him. He's wanted down Texas way."

"As if," Kelly breathed, "you didn't know that when you made him your deputy."

Ignoring him, Rio rapped, "I'll take custody of the man, Gamble. Right now."

"I don't reckon," Badger said as flatly, "that you will."

"You're aidin' and abettin' a known criminal, Gamble. I'm warning you not to interfere."

"If keeping him locked up for a federal marshal is aidin' and abettin' him, then that's just what I'm doing."

A warning sense had stirred in Kelly and grown big. Rio had not come here with any real hope of having

Durnbo turned over to him for the asking, badly as the man must want him. This talk about sheltering a known criminal—a status Rio had not bestowed upon Durnbo until it suited his purpose—seemed to carry a hidden, a sinister significance.

Then Bell clarified matters considerably.

"If I got to come and take him by force," he rasped, "I will. And the rest of you with him, if you give me any more trouble."

He turned his horse and rode out.

It was a moment afterward before anybody spoke. "That was a piece of skulduggery," Croner said then. "But just how?"

"He told you himself," Kelly said harshly. "He branded us as criminals, didn't he? For refusing to give Durnbo up to the so-called law. And he knows we won't ever do it without a fight."

"So next," Badger said worriedly, "we get that fight."

"He must of been to Horse Track," Croner reflected, "and found out he got in plenty Dutch. But now he can go back and show Comber that he's the one man in this country that can kill off a few nesters in the name of the law."

"And Comber'll be plenty interested," Badger agreed.

"There's only one way outta the thing," Jim said from the doorway. "And that's for the sheriff's office to be vacated again real quick."

"Jim, don't try it," Kelly snapped.

Jim didn't reply.

"Well, we still got Durnbo," Badger reflected, "and it's time we put him to work for us."

"How?" Kelly asked.

"Let's pay him a visit and see."

They walked over to the stable, where Badger unlocked the padlock on the cooler door. When Durnbo came out he blinked his eyes against the stronger light, and he looked uneasy. The talk hadn't been loud enough for him to hear through the thick sod walls. He didn't know what was coming.

CHAPTER 18

BADGER GAVE HIM A LONG, COLD STARE. "YOUR OLD boss was just here," he reported. "Said you were wanted in Texas and wanted to arrest and take you in. We decided against it at the moment."

Durnbo looked puzzled, worried.

"What do you think would happen if we took you in to him ourselves?" Badger asked. "That he'd turn you loose as soon as he got you out of our hands? Me, I don't think he would. I figure the son would feel easier now if he knew you were dead and buried in that quicksand sink. It's damned easy for a rotten lawman to pull off a murder in the line of duty, you know."

Durnbo's cheeks had paled. He knew Bell's nature as well as Badger did. "What you gettin' at?" he grunted.

"Mebbe I'm going to offer you a choice. Between being turned over to Rio or to a U. S. Marshal."

"Where've I got a choice?"

"If you told everything you know about this rotten business it would sure spike Rio's guns and give you a chance to stay alive. I figure he'd turn around and try to pass the buck to Comber. That makes you a mighty important man, Durnbo. You want to stay alive on our side or die on his?"

Trench Durnbo made a hard swallow. "What kind of

charges you gonna make against me if we go to the federals?"

"Everything you're guilty of. But that way you get a trial. The other way a piece of Bell's lead."

"I'll go," Durnbo agreed. "And don't think I can't fix them two's wagons plenty. Comber paid me to get rid of Terry Kilrain. We was supposed to get rid of his daughter, too, but Drake drove us off. Bell shot Charlie Redd hisself to get that badge. I sat in when that was rigged up. Nobody but him seen it, but it was Bell told us to get Corb Rivers and Tansy Wooden and make another try for Abbie Kilrain. Believe me, I know plenty that either one would beef me for, now, I guess."

Badger was grinning when he snapped the padlock on Durnbo's prison again. As he left the stable with Kelly, he said, "That monkey knowed I wasn't foolin' about what Bell'd do to him. Funny about that breed. They distrust each other worse than the law they spend their lives mocking."

"When you going to take him in?"

"Soon as I can get started."

"You'll need help."

"That'd be smart," Badger agreed. "And I figured to ask Jim to come with me."

"So you realize he figures it's his job to vacate the sheriff's office."

"Which won't do."

"I sure agree with you there."

"Meanwhile," Badger reflected, "you better take Linda and the boy over to Abbie's to stay till I can get back."

But Kelly heard only a part of that. Twisting around, he stared at the horse corral.

"Jim!" he shouted. "What you doing on that bronc?"

163

Jim sat his saddle and was ready to ride out. His eyes were narrow slits as he stared at Kelly and Badger. They were completely unyielding and dangerous. A slow man to rile, he was a hard one to stop once he had started moving.

"Don't try to stop me," he warned. "For your own good. Bell's heading for Horse Track right now. I aim to see he don't get there."

"Jim, you stubborn—!"

"Leave be, Kelly. That man's going to pick up a posse on Horse Track. Probably he'll deputize every damned varmint. That's why he went to all the trouble warning us to expect arrest. He wants us in a fighting mood when he gets here with his picked posse. Man, stand outta my way. There ain't any time to lose."

Jim swung his horse, dug spurs and was gone.

"He was right about that posse," Kelly said. "That's Rio's comeback try. If he gets going with a crooked bunch of deputies, none of us has got a chance."

"Where you going?" Badger asked.

"After Jim. But you get on with your own job. We're going to need all the help we can get."

Kelly roped a fresh horse and saddled hastily. He had guessed much of Rio's plan, but not the full extent the way Jim had. Then Jim had wrapped the whole thing up together in the score he yearned to settle with Rio. Kelly didn't want to cross his friend. But Linda, in what she had once said about it, had been right. Rio was a trained killer, while Jim was not. And there were many more people than Jim involved in the matter.

Riding out from Running Iron, Kelly gave up any thought of trying to follow Rio's direct course. He knew the whole country better than Jim did. If he went straight to Abbie's place and headed north from there,

164

he might intercept Rio before Jim could overtake him. That was his best chance of doing any good.

He had picked a strong, long-legged horse that could eat up the miles. Even then, it seemed all too long before he was running down into the little bowl that sheltered Abbie's place. The driving beat of hoofs brought her into the yard, along with Colorado.

"What now?" Abbie moaned when she saw Kelly's tight face.

He told them briefly what had happened, what they now had to meet. He saw the shock of Abbie's brown features give way to a deep and moving fear.

"Where are you going?" she asked.

"There's a chance I can head Rio off before he gets to Horse Track. And before Jim can overtake him."

"You've got to!" she breathed. "Don't let Jim go up against that trained killer, Kelly!"

He stared at her in sharp wonder. The urgency and concern in her voice were tearingly real. Had a Texas man got through to her at last, a gentle, patient, kindly one like Jim? He saw the answer, stark and unashamed in her eyes. Her days here with Jim had done something to Abbie, as had her days with little Jimmy.

"I won't," he promised, and then was riding again.

He kept on west, arriving at the place where he had started out on his long tracking, when he had kept Jim from meeting death in the quicksand sink. It was probably as straight a route as any, and would lead him to Horse Track headquarters.

He felt that he stood a fair chance of heading Rio off. That was as important as keeping Jim from meeting the man Linda had once loved. If Comber and the hardcases he again controlled ever got the sanction of the law

165

behind them, however spurious, blood would run deep on the range.

The country through which he traveled swiftly had a familiar look this time. Although the wind had done its erasing work, he now and then saw some of the sign he had followed once before. The air still stirred, bringing with it the smells of nature in all its rawness and now more of the cooling of autumn. His horse ran with steady speed.

When he reached the rim from which, once before, he had looked down upon Horse Track headquarters, he saw nothing but a scene of complete serenity. That was encouraging. If Rio had reached here, they would be rushing about. Comber would be eager to act on the new situation the sham sheriff had created in hopes of winning his way back into favor.

Kelly pulled back a short distance to cut himself off from sight of the place. Afterward he sat motionless in the leather, studying the sweep of terrain that rolled so vastly on his right. If he and Jim were right in their initial surmises, Rio would be cutting a tangent across that country now. He would show up out there presently or-it would mean that Jim had overtaken him.

Kelly allowed the horse only a few minutes rest, then drove it to the southeast. He rode warily for the country itself was deceitful and tricky. What looked like a continuous flat would prove on close approach to contain concealed hollows. As the hills wheeled back, solid masses broke into many bewildering ravines that could be traveled.

When he sighted his man it was with the complete unexpectedness that he had watched against so closely. A rider loped around the fat ankle of a butte and instantly hauled down his horse. Recognizing the color of the animal and the general shape of the rider, Kelly knew at once who it was.

Rio Bell was the more puzzled, not knowing if Kelly was somebody from Horse Track, where he still had not squared himself, or an even more deadly enemy from the nesters. Kelly rode steadily toward him, hoping that Rio would let him come in pistol range. But driving urgencies crowded the man. He did not mean to let anything turn him from his main course. He pulled the horse about and rode hastily behind the cover of the low headland.

That forced on Kelly the need for a quick, radical decision. He dared not follow the man and yet could not give him a chance to cut around and reach Horse Track. He considered Rio's unwillingness to be pinned down at this point and decided to make what use he could of it.

He swung his horse in on the other side of the long earth talus, then urged it quietly up the slant. He came over the top very cautiously and saw below him a waiting horse, the rider carefully watching the end of the point. Then, as his horse alerted, Rio again dug spurs. This time he was forced by Kelly's position to ride straight onto the open plain, but on a tangent that led away from Comber's headquarters.

Kelly drove out after him in bold and stubborn chase, cutting to Rio's left and pressing him steadily away from Horse Track. It was like running a wild horse, which in a sense was what Rio was. Kelly knew his own mount was the stronger, if not the swifter. He bent himself now to keep Rio from reaching Comber and help, intent on running him down and forcing him to make a stand.

Rio did not catch onto that purpose immediately, might not yet have determined whether his pursuer came from Horse Track or elsewhere. He was bent low on his horse, quirting it desperately from side to side, and in so doing was rapidly using up his reserve strength. Once, as if beginning to collect his wits, he tried to swing back toward Comber's but again Kelly headed him off. The frenzy with which he belabored the horse showed that Rio Bell was getting scared.

When Bell cut sharply to the right, bearing for the cover of the hills, Kelly again headed him back into the open. Steadily they increased the distance between themselves and the place Rio hoped to reach. By now Rio knew who was after him, Kelly judged. He was not sure of his ability to withstand a gunfight; he had too much at stake to want to risk it now. He knew as well as Kelly did that his horse was badly worn down.

For another five minutes they rode steadily, and Kelly thought that he now had the ability to close the gap and force the showdown. But at that moment Rio dropped from sight as if the ground ahead had opened up to swallow him.

Put to a snap decision, Kelly bent left as he topped the rise. But Rio had been cunning enough to take the opposite direction along the hollow, moving farther away from Horse Track. He'd bet on Kelly's skirting the hollow safely for some distance before daring to show himself.

Rio had widened the distance between them, even so, but now he was committed to the stand he had tried so hard to avoid. Yet he would hunt his own place for it, He had soon vanished into the hills.

As long as he could see the horse tracks ahead of him, Kelly kept riding. Yet a bright, brittle tension now stood in him that the least outward disturbance could explode into premature action. When he saw from the hoof prints that Rio had slowed down, or that the horse had played out, Kelly swung from the saddle.

Leaving his mount, he moved up onto the hill.

CHAPTER 19

PRESENTLY HE SAW RIO'S HORSE BELOW HIM, SWEAT-soaked and heaving and ready to collapse. Kelly grinned in cold humor but was not oblivious of the fact that if Rio back-tracked and got his Running Iron horse, the tables would be turned abruptly. He watched steadily against that chance, although presently the boot prints pointed on up the hollow. As he moved on Kelly kept his present elevation.

The ravine climbed for a time, was still too bare of cover to interest Rio in halting. Soon Kelly saw below and ahead of him a small clump of brush. Water seeped from this edge and ran a distance before losing itself into the sandy soil. It was some kind of weak spring, the only cover so far found, and Kelly knew where his enemy was at that moment. The far rise was more abrupt than previously. The area below was obscured by deep shadows. It was quiet except for the stirring of the air.

Then Kelly went down hard and flat as a pistol shot rang out.

The bullet had come so close to him he had heard it pass. His breathing all but stopped. But as he had judged, there was enough swell in that slope that, flattened out, he could see only the top of the brush growing about the seep. That and nothing more, yet Kelly knew that within minutes he or Rio Bell would die. He began to inch downward. The silence was as deadly as if they had been the only two men remaining in a desolate world.

Then came Rio's voice.

"Drake—do we have to finish this?"

169

That was the first time Kelly had ever found satisfaction in his reputation as a gunmaster. Like so many creatures of his kind, Rio lacked the nerve to meet a man his deep uneasiness told him was his better. This lonely kind of death carried humiliation with it. Before onlookers he would have found more courage. Now there was no one to watch. He was willing to back-track a little.

"Got an offer, Rio?" Kelly called.

"Well, can't we talk it over?"

"Not this side of hell."

A sudden suspicion had come to Kelly. Maybe Rio had been using the cover of his talk to move into a better position for his stand. Pulling off his hat, Kelly laid it on the ground as far out as he could reach, then began to push it as he crawled.

A gun exploded twice, although it was almost a single sound. The hat rolled backward, kicked-up dust rising there. Like a released spring, Kelly was on his feet. He was just far enough over from the place Rio watched to make it.

Rio had come out of the brush. There had been a look of eagerness on his face until shock washed it off. He had only a little way to swing his pistol. Again Kelly seemed to hear but a single, crashing outburst of sound although he knew his own gun thundered with Rio's. He felt no impact. Instead, he saw Rio's body bow backward. Rio's fingers relaxed to let the gun fall a second before he went down. That was the last motion he could make.

Kelly stood there a moment, sick and shaken. Then he moved slowly down to where Rio lay. He reached down and unpinned the star from Rio's vest . . .

He had confused himself greatly by the zigzag course he had ridden in the grim chasing of Rio. But now he

170

could be more sparing of his horse as he began to follow his own backtrail. The star was in his pocket where it had no legal right to be, but he felt he had every moral right to carry it there. He decided to go back to Running Iron and wait for Badger's return. He would follow Rio's trail, in hope of finding out what had happened to Jim.

He had just cut the trail Rio had taken, after leaving Badger Gamble's, when he saw two riders coming along that same trail toward him. All three of them pulled down their horses for a moment, studying one another.

Yet one of those horses was Badger's, and the only thing puzzling Kelly was why Badger should be coming this way when he had intended to leave with Trench Durnbo. Then he was sure that the man with Badger was Jim. Kelly waved his hat above his head, then the three of them came together on the trail.

Badger carried a battered old book under his arm.

Kelly reached in his pocket and pulled out the sheriff's badge, which he handed to Badger. Looking at Jim, he said, "I hope you take it right, Jim. But I figured that one snake was mine to kill."

Jim looked at the badge with a dark gleam in his eyes. Then he nodded.

"He wouldn't close with me. Just outrun me."

"Then you were a big help to me," Kelly said. "Because I had to finish playing out his horse before he'd corner. I reckon his not caring to face you was some satisfaction to you."

"Enough," Jim agreed. There seemed to be relief in him, now, that he had not done the thing that would have stood forever between him and Linda.

"I sent Pete and Nick with Durnbo," Badger said

171

then. "This thing just wouldn't keep long enough for me to go. Even with Bell outta it, we've got Comber riding high in the saddle."

"What can you do about him?"

"I figured," said Badger with a thin grin, "it was time me and old Chance had a little business meeting."

"If you're going to Horse Track, I'm going with you."

"Come along," Badger agreed. I reckon I could stand a little more backing."

Badger didn't seem talkative, letting Kelly and Jim guess what he had in mind. They rode on toward Comber's headquarters.

The unusual number of men kept in at Horse Track, when they should have been off working, showed that Chance Comber was plotting a move of some sort. Although Kelly had undergone a great deal since he had last seen the man, there in the dawn at the line camp, those triumphs were still fresh and glowing in the mind of Comber.

When the three nesters came into the yard they created an immediate stir. The daring of it was of sufficient cogency to turn the Horse Track men uncertain and cautious. They sat around the bunkhouse door, a couple on the steps of the big house. Badger kept to the saddle when he pulled down in front of the latter pair.

"Chance here?" he asked.

"He's here," a man grunted.

"Tell him to come out. I aim to have a powwow. You all better be in on it."

The man looked surly, but be rose and climbed the steps. A moment after he had gone into the house, Comber came out. Bewilderment showed on his face, a quick hostility. Badger reached into his shirt pocket,

172

fished a little, and brought out the sheriff's star.

Including the other men, who had gathered around, Badger said, "We'll start off with this little trinket. It's going to take a good polishin' before it'll be fit for a white man to wear again."

One of the staring men blurted out the question that had sprung into the minds of all.

"What the hell happened to Rio?"

Badger's mouth made a mirthless grin.

"Don't figure he'd surrender the thing voluntarily, do you? He's out in the hills. Coyote bait. Not that it grieves any of you much. What will is the sorry fate of Trench Durnbo. By now he's well on his way outta this country. And some eager to spill all he knows to the federal officers about Comber's land-grab scheme and the killings that came out of it."

Chance Comber's eyes opened wide at that. He shot a desperate look about him but got no comfort from his men. Comber had hired special killers. They were thinking of that, figuring their own chances of keeping in the clear.

In turn Badger stared long at Comber. "Been a long while," he said, "since there was a cow outfit called Gamble and Comber. Lot of your riders don't know there ever was such a firm. That it was me who gave Chance Comber his start in the business then got double-crossed out of everything."

Kelly could see that this was news indeed to most of the intent listeners. However long they had ridden for Horse Track, they had lived with the understandable idea that Badger Gamble was nothing more than a tough, clever old cattle rustler.

Badger took the book he had carried under his arm and held it up in his good hand.

173

"Take a look at this old account book of mine, Chance. It shows where you and Zigzag and M Bar have been given full credit, at going prices, for every steer we ever took from any of you. Received on account, it says. It's all pretty close to squared up now. So we'll call it quits."

"Well, now—" Comber began. He seemed to hope that a peace offer was coming.

"But there's something," Badger rapped, "that you never can square. For the men you've killed or had killed. Terry Kilrain—Charlie Redd—Corb Rivers—all friends of mine."

Comber made an audible gasp as he understood Badger's meaning. The faces of his watching men showed plainly how far they had withdrawn from the situation, themselves. Again the cattleman stood all alone.

Comber read these things then acted on them in the one way his nature would let him. Badger had one arm in a sling, the account book in his other hand. Yet Comber stabbed down for the gun on his hip. As his fingers came out filled, Kelly's voice ripped in.

"Not a helpless man, Comber—not him!"

Comber slapped his gaze at Kelly. If anything, the enmity in his eyes increased. His gun was already riding in his hand above the bolster. Kelly's hand was empty. Yet the driving fears, the frustrations in Comber forced action, nothing less. With a growl he brought the gun on up, heeling toward Kelly.

Comber's hasty shot knocked the hat sailing from Kelly's head. But even as the man fired, Kelly's hand became full. A steady finger tugged on the trigger. Comber seemed to hiccough. He fell sprawling down the steps.

A set-faced Badger tossed the old account book down beside Comber. He turned his back disdainfully on the watching Horse Track riders. Kelly saw that none of them was going to take it up. He and Jim followed the old warrior.

Short of Badger's headquarters, Jim pulled down his horse, saying, "I reckon I won't be going back to Running Iron right now."

"Look, Jim—" Kelly began earnestly.

Jim gave him a slow, friendly smile that, for the first time in a great while, seemed to spring from some returned warmth within him.

"Me and Linda talked it all over, Kelly," he said. "We're friends again, but we both know that what used to be between us is gone once and for all. She asked me to get the knot cut, and I said I would."

"But the boy!" Kelly protested.

"She wants me to keep him. Under the circumstances, I guess it's best."

"You can't raise him by yourself!"

"Me," said Jim, with another grin, "I don't figure to try."

Then he was gone, cutting a slant to the southwest, toward Abbie's place. Kelly understood then, and a great, deep easing came to himself.

"I figured it would turn out this way," Badger said softly. "Once I got to know the four of you, I seen how life had sure scrambled your deck. Thank God there's plenty of people like Jim and Abbie in the world. Steady but tough as hell when they need to be, then settled and progressive again. Them two'll make good parents for a young and growing boy."

"But Linda—she can't just take off alone!"

"I hope, son, she don't have to try."

But Kelly had started his horse, forgetting Badger,

heading for Running Iron. The wind brushed his face, the fall sun was bright on the land, there was no cloud in all that sky.

Far off through the haze the horizons were calling, as they always had, as they always would. There had to be steady people in the world, and there had to be the adventurous, as well.

And even the adventurous ones needed their love at their sides . . .

We hope that you enjoyed reading this
Sagebrush Large Print Western.
If you would like to read more Sagebrush titles,
ask your librarian or contact the Publishers:

United States and Canada

Thomas T. Beeler, *Publisher*
Post Office Box 659
Hampton Falls, New Hampshire 03844-0659
(800) 818-7574

United Kingdom, Eire, and
the Republic of South Africa

Isis Publishing Ltd
7 Centremead
Osney Mead
Oxford OX2 0ES England
(01865) 250333

Australia and New Zealand

Bolinda Publishing Pty. Ltd.
17 Mohr Street
Tullamarine, 3043, Victoria, Australia
(016103) 9338 0666